Walking in Balance
Meeyau-ossaewin

Walking in Balance
Meeyau-ossaewin

Basil Johnston
O.Ont., LLD, B.A.

Kegedonce Press
Cape Croker Reserve, R.R. 5
Wiarton, ON Canada N0H 2T0

Walking in Balance © 2013 Basil H. Johnston

 Published by Kegedonce Press
Cape Croker First Nation,
P.O. Box 517, Owen Sound, ON N4K 5R1
www.kegedonce.com

Editor: Kateri Akiwenzie-Damm
Cover design : Adrian Nadjiwon
Inside Illustrations: Don Chrétien
Book design: Cynthia Cake, Wemakebooks.ca
Printed in Canada

Kegedonce Press gratefully acknowledges the generous support of:

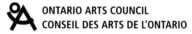

We acknowledge the support of the Canada Council for the Arts which last year invested $20.1 million in writing and publishing throughout Canada.

ONTARIO ARTS COUNCIL
CONSEIL DES ARTS DE L'ONTARIO

SALES AND DISTRIBUTION:
Literary Press Group of Canada
http://www.lpg.ca/
LitDistco: For Customer Service/Orders Tel 1-800-591-6250
        Fax 1-800-591-6251 Email orders@litdistco.ca
        8300 Lawson Rd., Milton ON L9T 0A4

Library and Archives Canada Cataloguing in Publication
Johnston, Basil, 1929– Walking in Balance / Basil H. Johnston; illustrated by Donald Chrétien.
Stories in English and the Anishinaabe languages.

ISBN 978-0-9868740-4-8 (pbk.)
1. Ojibwa Indians--Religion. 2. Ojibwa philosophy.
3. Conduct of life. I. Title.

E99.C6J686 2013   299.7'8333044   C2013-907888-6

CONTENTS

WINONAH

I am Winonah, daughter of Nookoomiss. I should call her N`gushih really but like everybody in our village I too call her "Nookoomiss," a term of respect for elder women who are kind and forgiving and ready to share what they know with children. Besides sharing what they know with the young they help young mothers care for their babies.

Grandmothers make sure that their grandchildren don't touch snakes or eat poisonous plants or wander off with the dog. Grandmothers are watchful that children don't play dangerous games such as running about with burning sticks or going too far out into the water. To make their point the grandmothers tell their grandchildren how 'One Eye' lost his other eye when he was playing war with other boys – they were using blunt headed arrows. They told about a boy who thought it was great fun to run around an outdoor fireplace and jump over it. "Don't do that! You might trip and fall into the fire!" That is what happened. He tripped. He fell into the flames. The people and the boy screamed and sparks leaped overhead. The boy lived but, for years afterward, nightmares haunted his every sleep.

Stories about humans, acted out by humans, tell about life, about what we should do and what we should not do. Mother Earth teaches, she shows. Children and adults only have to watch and listen to insects, birds, animals, fish, and plants to learn how to live in harmony, to get along with neighbours. And as grandparents tell stories, children learn language, enrich their imaginations and rouse their curiosities about the herebefore and the hereafter.

Stories don't need special occasions or times to be told. The tellers do not say, "Now I'm going to tell you a children's story," as if there were different intellectual levels of stories. It was children who had to uplift, improve, and upgrade their understandings. Work-time was as good a time as any to pass on what listeners wanted to know. When grandmother gets out birch bark, quills, pigments or scrapes deer hide on its frame, children watch; they all want to know why she is doing what she is doing.

"Watch!" grandmother would say. "Watch how I do it! Someday you're going to do this."

In another part of the village the old men were busy making a canoe; at another time they would be webbing snowshoes, steaming black ash, or making bows and arrows.

By watching our grandparents make tools and clothing, and assemble birch bark for our homes, we learn which furs are good for what, which trees are good for what and best for cutting down. We went with them when they went gathering for medicine plants, drying them and putting them away for use later.

We learned where these plants and trees grew, which birds and insects fed upon which trees and plants. From watching and listening to our parents and grandparents we learned what they admired in neighbours. The Anishinaubae people: a hardworking people, a reflection of themselves, who detested laziness. For us young women, a hard working man was to be sought; for young men a good natured woman would bring happy days.

Our elders did not need to say certain things. They let their conduct and habits and living in harmony with the land and the seasons tell better than any man could what is patience, diligence, self-control, endurance, and all traits needed to live a life as a hunter and fisher armed with but a bow and arrow and awl and scrapers.

From the time that I was eight years old until I was about fifteen Nookoomiss told me that when I was going to empty my bladder to make sure that no one saw me in my nakedness. When I asked "why?" she explained that there were men and even Manitous prowling about looking for women flaunting their maidenheads. I took care to keep out of sight whenever I needed to spill water.

One day, some years later, when I was a young woman out with a company of friends picking strawberries, I had to spill water. My companions and I were competing to see who could pick the most berries and I did not want to fall behind. Not wanting to lose, I ran into the nearest thicket unmindful of prying eyes to spill water. It was then that Ae-pungishimook, the Spirit of the West, seized and ravished me. When he had done with me he left to continue on his way.

Upon my return my companions wanted to know what had taken me so long. I hemmed and hawed that I was constipated.

A month later, Nookoomiss called me to her side and looked directly into my eyes without saying a word before she murmured, "you're going to have a child. Your eyes tell on you." She paused for a moment then asked: "Who did this to you?"

"Ae-pungishimook!" I answered, and then a torrent of tears fell.

"You're going to give birth to a Manitou's child!"

NANA'B'OOZOO OONDAUDIZIWIN

Gauwauhn w'gee gidizh-gaudaenih w'disseesm mee w'gee pagidinind w'missudauning w'gushiwun, w'gee dautig-aubumaut "Nana'b'oozoo n'zhinikauz!" w'gee kittoh.

W'gauh-apeetchih kishkoomikoot Winonah mee w'gee nikau-bundumaet, Chibwauh pungishimaut mitukumik w'd'odisseemun w'gee-nawudinikoon, W'ookoomissun-gee kitchi-weekinaumoowun, w'gee neenimi-kaudaessaewun gayae "Awaenaen dano'oh naubae w'gauh oondaudizee-ut agid-kumik" w'gee gagawadedjimaun w'daunissun.

W'wee nanaugizo-waubumaun w'ozhi-shaehn gomauminik w'abee-aut gaego washamae tchi w'kittonit, kauween dush gaego w'gee kittoos-seewun. Kishkumauk-doonaenih aetah-tibishko gageebinakawaet.

Chibwauh tibikuk mee gee kikaendaugook abi-inoodjeehnse w'gau-keegitoot, bidjeenuk w'gauh oondaudizit, w'gee weendum-oowaun ookoomissun "Nana'b'oozoo n'd'izhinikauz." Gaegaet w'gauh apeetauni kidoonaessaewaut Anishinaubaek dibaudjimauwaut oshki abi-anoodjeehnsun.

Aunind bim-gaedauguniwaun w'geekishkoomiwaemik-oowaaun." Auyauh! Kauween igoh nauh gonamauh! Kauween abi-anoodjeehnsuk geekittoosseewuk paumauh neezhoo-abi-boonikuk ashi-aupta gauh kabik-issaemiguk, apeetchin nawutch weekauh.

Keeshpin gauh izhi-waebutoogawaen, kauween onishishisseenoon; neezho-abi-booninugizit owih abi-anoodjeehnse. Mee suh w'ae-izhi-waebuzit awiyah anoodjeekaugoot manitoun; gonamauh mindimooyaehnuk w'gauh pitchi-nauwaugawaenun.

Kauween goshah ween, W'd'odisseemun w'gee noondoowaun, w'ookoomissun gayae. Meenwauh gayae aupitchih igoh nauh w'gee gootaudjimaewizih-tibishko... odjidumoh... gausk-gausk-naudjeehn.

Gauh ishkawauh ondaudizit Nana'b'oozoo kauween ginowaesh gee auwizeenoon mee gee nibonit w'gushiwun, Winonah. Ahneesh mee suh aubidaek Nookoomiss gee kooginaut, Nana'b'oozoon, nishkae.

Ahneen gonamauh gae izhitchigaepun? W'bim-gaedaugoonun w'gee abi-naudimaukoon, abeedumaukoot meedjiin, gawiwinun, mashki-aki, waegeedoogawaen w'maenizigawaen Weedji-quaewun gee abi weedookoowauwaun abi-anoodjeehnsun tchi zhaugooskuminit w'd'gootaudj-naewizinwin. Apee w'gauh ningut-aenimaut manitoushaehnsun, benaessiwun, waesseehnun, waegawaenisheedoogaenuk naen-nawjautoonigawaenun neebautibik, maegayauk.

Ningot-wauss abi-boon-igizeeban Nana'b'oozoo maegawawautch apee w'gauh gagaedjimaut w'ookoomissun w'aeyaunit w'neegee-ikoon.

"Gee maudjauwuk," aetah w'gauh kittoot.

"Oohn!"

Ningoting neegaun nakae washamae w'dah nindo kiki-aenimaun ahneen meeyow w'gauh w'izhi-waebuzinit w'kitizeemun. Tchi awunushkawaezimaut ozhishaehnun mindimooyaehn w'gee mukowaumaun weebah auwuninik tchi awo-gawishimoot tibishko kakinah ininiwuk w'gauh doodum-oowaut tchi w'ininiweewiwaut. W'dauh wizheetauh tchi dae apeet-aendaugozit tchi-w'gawishimoot, tchi 'naugadoot bimaudizi-meekunuh-tchi meeyoow-ossaet.

"Aundih aen-imook bimaudizi-meekunuk?" Nana'b'oozoo gagawaedjimaun ookoomissun.

"Awo-gagaedjim aki-waezheeshishuk."

Nana'b'oozoo w'gee izhaumaut kaetizinit.

Aen dasso geezhiguk w'gee awo-kik-noowautchitoon gawishimoot metig-wauk akeeng. Ayae-oshkut w'gee oombauwae-igoon, weebah dush w'gee zhigud-aendaun. Weebah dush gee izhissaemigutinik Nana'-b'oozoo tchi w'gawishimoot. Kauween dush w'gee wizhee-awosseebun.

Nookoomiss w'gee noondaeshkoowaun Nanan'b'oozoo wizheetausseenik apee w'gauh nindo-waewaemaut "ahow! Mee auzhigoh

izhissaemiguk tchi gawishimooyin! Nanan'b"oozoo gee giniskauwi-
kunaeshkauh naningauk-ozidaeshkauh w'gauh apee tchi-zaegizit.
W'gee ayau-waendum" N'maunmundjiw" w'kittoh.

"K'zaegis nah?" w'd'ikoon ookoomissun.

Kauween.

Ahneen waenaen dush bayaubeetooyin? Ani-maudjaut, Kauween
gagawaedjumisseenoon tchi indaendiyin gomau-minik dasso-goon,
kemauh waussah, kemauh maegawauh gootaumigook, Kauween
zaum waussah K'wee izhin-izhoowisseenoon, daebinauk igoh tchi
daebitooyin. K'gah weendumoon apee gae noogish-kauyin.

Gaegauh Nana'b'oozoo w'kaudun w'geezhoobaukishkaunoon
w'wee ningunaut w'ookoomissun, ween dush tchi nishikaewizit
metigauk-akeeng aundih w'gauh daneewaut mishi-ginaebeegook,
manitouk, subkaesheek baubeewikoot. Kauween washamae neezh
tunnuh dasso-ozid w'gee izhaussee Nanan'b'oozoo, mee gee noog-
ishkaut w'gee beebaugimaut w'ookoomissum "Noko! Mee nah dae
waussuh!"

Kauween! Keeyaubih! K'waubmin goshah?"

Nana'b'oozoo w'gee ani-kooshkawae-ossae-kummee; baeshoh
igoh nauh izhauh, mee meenawauh w'gee noog-gauboowit mee w'gee
gazheewaemaut w'ookoomissun. "Mee nah dae-waussah?"

Keeyaubih goshah k'waubmin! Kegoh noogishkaukaen paumauh
nakaewaeshkawiyin. Awuss!"

Ketwaen Nana'b'oozoo w'gee maud-kaudae-ossae, tibishko
mishee-kaehning ae-apeeskaut w'gee apeeskauh-ani-apeeskaut, w'gee
bizozidaeshin cheebikaeshing, geesh kunutoong; w'gee bauzigoh-
anikaeshin; w'gee chee-cheesh-kaudaeshin assineeng, tikwanaung,
baug-kummik-gaunik. Gomau-apeetch w'gee nabaek-issae waun-
kummik-gaunik, aundih gauh dazhi-bim-aungizoot; kauween w'gee
waubumausseen ookoomissun, kauween gayae w'gee waubu-
mikoosseen.

Nana'b'oozoo w'gee gawaek-quaenih awuss nakae w'gee
inausseengwaeshing mee dush w'gee gazhee-waewaemaut
w'ookoomissun "Dae wussuh nah noongoom?"

"Gonamauh! Kauween K'waubumeessinoon! Kegoh ningodjih d'zhaukaen. Mee igoh omauh ayaun!

"Ahow!"

"Ahow!" w'geekittoowun kauween dush w'gee daeb waewaenduzcc Nanan'b'oozoo w'gauh apeetchih zaegizit. Apee gauh autaenik ishkotae boodawaun mee Nana'b'oozoo w'gee cheeng-nubit tchi w'zhaeodaet naeyaub w'ookoomissun 'w'ae-indaunit-washamae baeshoh.

Chibwauh mook-waussigaet geezis gizhaeb waussayaushk-kung kakinah gaego Nanan'b'oozoo w'gee piskau-odae gauh dazhi nebaut, waun-kummikaunik, mee igoh paubigae w'gee ani-nebaut. Paumauh w'gee kishkoozih w'gauh mudjikoot ookoomissun "How! Winishkaun! Kauween k'dauh abi-boonishingwaumissee. K'pakadaetnaudoog!

Kidimaugiz! K'd'ayaekizinaudoog!

Dae-minik dasso-geezis gee kabik-issae mee minik mindimooyaehn w'gee mukwo-aenimaut w'ozhishaehnun gauh gawishimoonit.

"N'gee awo-gawishim, kauween dush gaego'gee baewuduzeen.

"N'kik-aendaun."

"Ahneesh ae-izhi-kik-aendumun? Waendesh w'gauh weendumaukiyin?"

Benaeskeehnsuk n'gee weendumaukook w'gee nebausseewun k'missud n'gee weendumaukoon pakadaeyin; k'chiboam, k'doodaem, w'nindo-waendaunauwauh tchi bawaudjgaenit Nana'b'oozoo tch weedji-akiwaemikoowaut manitoun, tchi dittumoowaut ae-izhi daeb-naewiziwaut.

Nawuch w'gauh ani-kitchi-auwit Nana'b'oozoo washamae w'gee sub-audji-ayauh tchi 'weedji-aki-waemaupun manitoun, tehi minonawaemikoot w'gee masedissaunun aen-daneenit zhawaendaugizinit. Aubiding w'gauh izhaut aen daneenit manitoun. W'ayaekoozit w'gee awo-gawishimoh. Neezhi-goon kaween gaego w'gee meedjisseen. Aen-dasso geezhiguk wauwaushkaeshiwuk w'gee baeshowitaukoon. W'gauh w'inaendung pakadaekaepun mee suḥ w'gee bimoowautt baezhig wauwaushKaeshiwun. Kitchi wauweesinih geewaehn beenish gee mooshkinutoot w'missud, mee dush gee ani-nebaud.

"Ahneen! K'gee bawaudjigae nah?" Nana'b'oozoo w'gee gaga-waedjimikoon w'ookoomissun apee w'gauh peendigaewaut ae-indau-waut. Gaegaet! Nana'b'oozoo w'gee maumeek-waudjimoh. Kauween w'gee bawaudjigaessee; w'gee bawaunaun waendjidah mukwon, migiziwun, myeengunun, iskotae-benaessiwun, misheekaehn w'gee odissikoon w'abeedumaukoot ayawaumitoowau-waumoowin, mino-waubinzaewiziwin gayae.

"Apaegish! N'ozhi-shaehnse! Dayaebiwaewinaen!" kittoowun w'ookoomissun.

MAUDJEE-KAWISS

Nine months after Ae-pungishimook had made her a mother Winonah gave birth to a boy. She called him Kawiss.

Only after Kawiss was born did his father come back to see what kind of son he had gathered. In his dreams Ae-pungishimook saw his son as a great hunter and warrior – a man who kept their caches filled with meat and who kept many warriors away from their homes. This was not Winonah's dream; a hunter yes, but not a warrior meant to go on raids to kill or himself be killed, or to be crippled for life unable to look after her in her old age.

As soon as Kawiss was able to walk, Ae-pungishimook made him a toy bow and arrow and club. With these weapons Kawiss practiced marksmanship and with exercises, built up his strength and endurance.

By the time that he was seven years old Kawiss was bigger, faster, and stronger than any man in the village, perhaps in the nation. It was unbelievable. He now spent most of his time in his father's company leaving his mother alone to worry about his well-being. She often complained that "My spirit and soul and heart go wherever you go, watching over you, seeing to it that nothing evil happens to you."

Kawiss was not quite fifteen when he began to venture alone into territories that belonged to other peoples. On one of his first visits he came upon a gathering of headmen who invited him to take in their discussions.

For the first time Kawiss saw something that he'd never seen or heard of: speakers with sashes draped over their arms on which were woven symbols that the speakers pointed to during their speeches. Other than uttering the occasional "How! How!" the audience did not interrupt the speakers, such was their respect of words and speech and good manners.

During a break in the meeting Kawiss asked what the sashes were for. "Oh!" one of the headmen exclaimed. "We call it waumpum. It's a history of our peoples; it records what we have accomplished and where we have fallen short; it keeps in our minds where our rituals came from and what they mean, and our sense of equality; it reminds us of our rights and duties, and of our seeking to live up to the meaning of Anishinaubae, a person who means to abide by the spirit of living in harmony. The waumpum sash as a history gives us pride as well as humility. Do you have anything like this to keep your traditions in your memories?" the headman asked Kawiss, extending the sash in the direction of Kawiss as if inviting Kawiss to take it in his hand to examine it.

Believing that he was meant to hold the sash and to look it over, Kawiss took the sash in his hand. The moment that Kawiss touched the waumpum sash, the crowd gasped. "He's touched our totemic scroll. Get him! Make him run the gauntlet!"

So startled was Kawiss that he ran off with the sash, the crowd shouting and calling for his blood and his life.

Before he had gone far, Kawiss stopped in his tracks to face his pursuers with his club. With one swing of his club Kawiss knocked the brains out of his nearest pursuer. When the pursuers heard the skull crack and saw the brains fly, they stopped short and began to circle Kawiss.

Not far behind were the elders crying out, "Don't kill him. We need him. He has slain our chief warrior."

At their Elder's telling them to hold up, the warriors held up, grumbling, "But he killed our warrior chief … now we have no one to lead us."

"That's just it," the elder of the eldest added. "We need a war chief such as this man. It would be an honour to adopt this man into our community and to serve our people as head warrior."

"Would you be our head warrior?" the elders asked Kawiss.

"I'd be glad to lead your warriors," said Kawiss. Then he went on to explain who he was, where he came from, and that he would let his people know what he was about to do and ask his father's guidance.

Everyone agreed that for Kawiss to tell his parents and his people, and to ask their guidance was the proper thing to do. In return the Bear nation gave the idea of the sash to Kawiss to take back to his people.

The waupum sash is the legacy of Kawiss to our peoples. When his mother gave birth to another boy, Kawiss' name was changed to Maudjee-Kawiss, the Starting Son. Ever since it has been our people's custom to call the first son, Maudjee-Kawiss to commemorate his role as leader of a brother, or brothers – as a role model and safe guardian for his younger siblings.

Maudjee-Kawiss stands for action, deed, accomplishment, dream, guardianship, history, aspiration, defense, care model, and stoics.

MYEENGUNUK KIKI-NOOMOOWAUWAUN NANA'B'OOZOO

Nana'b'oozoo gee maudjauh, w'gee ningunaun w'ookoomissun nishikae tchi babau-aubundung ae-izhi-naugook w'd'akeemiwauh, aenigook-kawaukummigauk. Ishpi-tikwaugih auwunoobun apee Nana'b'oozoo gauh maudjaupun. Mee nitam w'gauh nishikaeweet.

Weekauh nishikaekumeesseek kauween Nana'b'oozoo w'gee kiki-aenduzeen aundih gae dazhi inukissitopun kabaeshiwin. Izhi bugwoonuh Nana'b'oozoo gee wizhigae nini-autikawau-akeeng gauh dazhi-dabinoowauseenook.

Gee bigum-aunimuk, mee igoh gayae w'gee maudj-poog. Nana' b'oozoo w'gee gaweeinwi-puto nindo-naeyung piskauk-inaendjigun boodaewaet, kauween dush gaego w'gee mukuzeen.

Mee dush maegawautch iwih apee, izhi-ningot-odaewizit myeen-gaungauhnsuk ishkawae koowauwaut w'gushiwaun. Myeengunuk w'gee goossauwaun Anishinaubaen iwih apee. W'gee noondoowau-waubuneen, mee dush noongoom nitam waubumaut "Kego goosau-kaegoon!" w'gee ikoowaun gushiwaun.

"Waenaesh keen?" Kitchi-myeengun gagawaedjimaun iniw naubaen.

"Nana'b'oozoo, n'd'izhi-inikauz."

"Needjee!" Wee bigumut ningodjih igoh nauh k'dauh gee wizhigae, aen-dazhi-dabinoowauk" Mee dush ae-izhi-ginoonaut w'needjaunissun." K'gah ne'b'aendawaunaun Nana'b'oozoo. Keeshpin w'beengaedjit, geezhoo-ozhaeshkoowik, Myeengauhnsuk gee geekishinook nawutch baesho goozhaewauwaut Nana'b'oozoon, zawaunikoomwaun, Weebah Nana'b'oozoo medawaewaedjaunaemooh. Kauween ginowaesh.

Anootch izhi-idjeeshimoh tchi bawi-waebishkung-kitchi-soossidum, chauchaumoh, gazhee waewaenaumoh "Phew!" Baekish gayae geezhoo-ozhaewooh" Ahnee gauh ondjih gazeebeeg-aunoo-waesseewaek, K'zoowaunokoomoowaun, Moowi-maugitoon, k'gee baumdaubaunauwaun moozoo-moowing. Mee igoh ae-izh-maug-ooziyaun gayae neen. Ningotchi w'gee izhi-waebishkung oozoowaunigooshun mee aundjih w'gee maudji-binigoot-naeyaub w'gee weekibidoot oozoowaunugooshun, gawozhaewoot meenwauh.

W'aen-waubung ae-datchiwaut myeengunuk Nana'b'oozoo gayae w'gee kooshkawae-osseek gooning gawaek geeshk-akeeng. Aubita-awoeeng w'gah dittimoowaut, w'noogi-ishkauwuk, w'gee dautig-quaeniwaut, w'gazheewaewaen-inaumook, nindo-maundijim aundigaewaut.

"Ahneen wae-ondjinin-doomaundjigaewaut? Gaegonah igoh?"

"Aehn! Wauwaushkaeshee-imaugaut. K'gah weesinim noongoom naukshik. Kauween nah gaego abeedji maunduzeen keen?"

"Kauween!" W'gee maenis-aendum Nana'b'oozoo nawutmaundjigaenit waesseehn ween dush, ningud-maundijaenit ween dush.

"Ahow! N'kawissdoog! Augawaumizik. Apeetchin aubnaubik. Gino-waubumishik, Mukwo-aendumook wauwaushkaeshiwuk noondumaewuk, ningud-maundjigaewuk gayae, kiki-aenimikaunik, babauayauying, cheegi-eeng; k'gah chaunimaeni-au-naun. Kauween kikiaenimikoosseenaun ae-aundih ae-ayauying. Kik-aendusseekoowauh aundih ae-ayauying, ae-chaunimaewiziwautch gae ani-ayaekiziwaut. K'gah naegautoonauwauh dush keeniwauh k'd'kishki-aewizi-winiwauh, gazheeb-inaewiziwininiwauh.

"Ae-gautch. Kegoh medawaewaetookegoon. Ahow! Umbae!"

Aundjih meeniwauh, w'gee maudjiwaut. Oshki-neegishuk nee gauneewuk meekunaukaewau-waut gushiwaun, Nana'b'oozoon gayae.

Gauh mukwo-aubumaut zaug-daeniniwae goodjininit w'kawissun, w'shazheeb-anauminit, gayae, w'gausk-anazootoowaun. "Kawae nawaebik!"

Meedush gee zhawaubeeg-ishinoowaut, gooning oshki-myee-gunuk kitchi wauweek-inaumoowuk. Gayae ween Nana'b'oozoo ani-chaugi-inaumoh, w'gawishimoh. Kauween ishi-baesho tchi noondi-windoowaubun.

"Needjee!" w'd'ikoon myeengunun. "Waenaen n'd'ooshkinee-gimuk aen-datchiwaut netau geewi-ossaet?"

Nana'b'oozoo w'gee naungizo-waubumaun oshki-neegi myeen-gunun, tibishko ninguz-aubumaut "Owih suh" izhi-inoowaut iniwih mayaumoowih ginowaunoowaenit.

"Ah, kauween needjee!" w'd'ikoon kitchi-myeengunun "Zaum keeyaubih waeweebinaewiih; mee igoh umbae weegawaushkini-toowaut; kauween ganagae pungee naungata-waenduzee. Kauween ginowaesh w'dauh dazheekaukosseen. Mee aetah tchi nawug-quaenit wauwaushkaesh, tchi-ombi-quaenit apee gawaushkinitaukoot myeen-gunun. W'ae-apeetchi-naewizit myeengun w'gee bizhibikoot wauwaush-kaeshiwun, kauween weekauh meeniwauh w'dauh dooduzeen. Meenwauh baezhig needjee.

Ae-iko neezhing Nana'b'oozoo w'gee dubug-aubunaun myeen-gunun, "Haw, waedih, mino-iniginoh."

"Kauween igoh nauh gonamauh! Zaum dah apaenimoondaun ae-inaubaewizit, ae-apeetcheeweet gaya, ae-apeetchi-putoot Gauwae-taunih weebah yaubae w'dauh maenishi-aun myeengunun anoo-kauzoot w'd'daeshkunun, w'ae'apeetch-pizoot gayae. Dubaub-oon meeniwauh.

Nissing meeniwauh w'gee weekitchitoon, nissing w'gee winissae. "Owih suh" kittoh myeenguni-quae izhinoowaut baezhig w'need-jaunissun, auptichih biziwaudiziwun, nishinaudji-beeyae tibisko igoh nauh w'gauh awo-tibidjeeshimoot weendjeeshkawa kaunik nongodjih. Ahneesh gae kishk-aewizipun owih dano-oh?

"Owih nah?" gagawaedawae Nana'b'oozoo auniwitung gauh waubundung.

"Aeh" nakawaetung myeenguni-quae.

"Ahneesh gae-izhi-zhaugooz-koowaupun weekaunaehnun wash-amae kaeshki-aewizinit?"

"Beewun!" K'gah waubumauh ae-izhi-kishki-aewizit.

Kauween gaego meeniwauh Nana'b'oozoo w'gee'kittoosee; kauween mino-minik w'gee kiki-aenduzeen tchi zhuegoozimaupun, W'gee daeb-waewaewaendum myeengunun daesdoo-waenimikoot tibishko buginoowizit; tibishko myeengauhnssuk washamae kish-ki-aewiziwaut tibishko waesseehnuk kiki-aendumoowut-kik-in-oomoowauwaut agidaudj-waesseehnun. Nana'b'oozoo w'gee weeskikaukoon daeb-waewaenimaut washamae, moon-aenimaut daes-doowaenimikoot. W'gee ishp-aenimoh, awiyah gee auwih, kishki-aewizhih. W'dah auzhidae-wauwaetoowaun. Anishinaubaek w'dah baup-auwaun myeegunun-gageebaudizidjik, baupinooza-waugunuk w'izhin- kaunauwaun.

PUKAWISS

Before there were books there was nothing to read; there being nothing to read, there were no schools; there being no schools, there were no teachers; there being no teachers, there were no classes.

Yet our ancestors learned not from books but from the greatest story teller and book they could have had. They had Mother Earth to show them what they needed and wanted to know.

Mother Earth presented her lessons as they were lived out in reality by bees, ants, butterflies, mosquitoes, worms, mice, spiders, flies; robins, seagulls, ravens, eagles sparrows, hawks, geese; bears, wolves, badgers, deer, caribou, moose, buffalo, chipmunks; bass, trout, muskellunge, perch, whitefish, catfish, minnows; sun, moon, rainbow, winds, storms, thunders, lightning; trees, grasses, leaves, vegetables, fruits, seeds, flowers.

All men and woman had to do was to watch, listen, touch, taste and smell, and use their minds. They will see the birth of a child and see its growth and watch it at play. They will listen to it sing or warble. The child will take in a sparrow coming to the defense of its babies and its nest and driving the attacker off; he will look on as ants, and insects, dismember a spider and then battle over the corpse; or he may see geese adopt baby geese as readily as if they were their own.

These happenings raise all kinds of questions.

When Pukawiss was born, Ae-pungishimook, the father, dreamed of another hunter warrior – this son would turn out to be a great hunter-warrior like Maudjee-Kawiss.

During the first two years of his life Pukawiss lived in a cradle-board, the whole of his world. They were his teachers. He listened and watched them and imitated them. Neighbours thought that this boy was an odd ball; that another spirit had entered his being, causing him to do what normal people would not do. But children his age went to watch him put on his acts. They found them funny. Even some adults found Pukawiss and what he was doing comical. At least it was harmless.

By the time that the boy was 15, his father had given up hope that his son would ever be a great hunter or warrior. He asked his son, "Where are you going? You're spending more time playing the fool than practicing your marksmanship. What are you doing?"

"I'm telling stories! I'm a story teller, Dad. I'm a teacher. I tell stories without words. I act out what I see taking place on the earth. I tell what insects, birds, animals, fish, and plants do; where they live; what they do and how they get along with each other. There are thousands of stories taking place every day on the ground, in the air, in the lakes and rivers.

In the fall I see seeds, nuts, and fruit drop to the ground. Mother Earth takes some of them into herself and feeds them. In the spring the seeds and nuts break through the crust of the earth as little green shoots and in a few days become flowers. About the same time, bees and ants by the millions come out of the earth as if by magic to care for the plants: fruits such as strawberry, blueberry, apple, and plum, and cherry and peach trees whose blossoms turn into hard little oval fruit; and vegetables such as leeks and corn.

Baby robins, hawks, eaglets, cardinals, chickadees, come into this world as eggs and live in nests under their parents' care and protection. The animals know what food is good for their offspring. Our ancestors and some older people call the animals our older brothers in the sense that they lead us, show us the way, and protect us.

Some of the most popular dances I've taught are: How the birds get their Colours, How the Crickets got their Dance, the Butterfly Dance, and the Rabbit Dance.

KEGO AUNOODIZIKAEN!

K'kitizeeminaubuneek naunigim k'gee aungawaum-mikoonaun "Kego zaum washamae mauwindoonigaen iwih dush gae daebissae-imbun. Washamae mizheenut meedjim aen-datchiying dush dah ishkossaemigut. Kakinah awiyah mino-minik w'dae itaenih meedjin, kauween maemikautch awiyah dauh pakadaessee. Keeshpin, aunind noondaessaewaut, babaumi-naundimoowaut dush, ween dindiwinoowauh. Kauween minik w'gee anookeeseewuk, zaum gee mino-pitaunauwauh newaebiwin, ae-apeet anookeewaut amauwundjitoowaut zeezibaukoot-auboo wauwauskoonae, sundjigoowaut gayae. Keeshpin aunind baemaudizidjik kitimaugiziwaut, mee kitimiwaut.

Missowauh w'gauh izheenoowaut benaehnsiwuk, waesseehnuk geegoohnuk, w'aen-dagowaugawaen geezhigoong, agid-kummik, gummeeng. Nana'b'oozoo w'd'aunoodiziwin w'gee dani-naundumook Kauween mino-minik w'gee ayauzeenauwauh wauh minozung w'wee shumauwaut w'needjaunissiwaun; w'gee nishki-aun Nana'b'oozoo weedigaemaugunun. W'gee gagauzoomaun "Tuguh! Ahneen w'ae ondjih weedjeewaussinuwoowauh k'weedji-ininiwuk wauwauhkaesheekaewaut, kemauh geegoohnkaewaut. N'd'ayaekpuwaunaun adjidumo, kookidjeesh, zhigaug, benaehn.

W'needjaunissiwaun w'gee naunaup-gauhnzoomauwaun ossewaun. "Ahneen aunind ininiwuk abi-akeewaewinauwaut wauwauhkaeshiwun. Waeshamae nah weeniwauh netau-geewi-ossaewuk?"

Kauween baezhig ae-izhi-neezhiwaut gaego w'gee kittooseewuk. Nana'b'oozoo gee maudjeegidauzoh.

Gumeeng Nana'b'oozoo gee waubumaun zhushigaun geegoohnkaenit. Nangae w'gee waenipushtoonauwauh, gawaubeeginauwaut geegoohnun. Ahneen gae izhi-geegoohkaewaupun aendaso-geezhiguk naussaub w'aen-anookeewaut, naussaub w'aeninundjigaewaut.

Nana'b'oozoo gee medwaewae-aubidaeshin ae-apeetchih kissinaunik. Mee igoh gayae w'gee geesaud-aendung w'gee bizinodwausseek weedigaemaugunun, neebinoong w'gee gauhnz-mikoot tchi awo-anookeet. Keeshpin bizindowaupun kauween noongoom w'dauh gee naning-gawauk-idjissee, Kauween.

"Ahneen! Needjee? K'dauh naudimow nah igoh. Kauween geegoohnuk goonduzeehnuk. Gonamauh shumoodjum mauzhpugidoodook. Gonamauh pakadaeesseedoogaenuk, gonamauh nunaudizidoogaenuk. Mundjih igoh nauh eedoog? Waeganae keen ae-anookauzeeyin?"

Zhushigauhgook gee dazhindaunduwauh aendoogawaen gae naudumoowauwaugaenun ae-izhi-geegookaewaut zhushigaugook tibikisko weeniwauh kemauh kego tchi baumaenimausseekoowauh bim-gaediginiwaun. Ween igoh w'doodaudizoh – maenoh dah weesikitoh ween gee abeedmaudizoh; aunind dush nawutch minodae-aewuk, abi-anoodjeehnuk mukwo-waenimaudauh, "zhaewaenumaudauh?" w'gee kittoowuk. Kauween k'dauh pshuzhaewausseenaun abi-anoodjeehnsuk ondjh w'kitizeemiwaun.

Kauween bizinduzee? Kitimishgh; daebi-naewizih noondaessaet.

Keeyaubih baezhig w'geekittoh "Keeshpin Nana'b'oozoo aetah daebaudjmauwingibun, kauween n'dauh naudimoowausee, ween gee doodaudizoh. Abi-anoodjeehnuk daebinaewiziwuk tchi-zhawaenimindoowauh. Zhawaenimaudauh! Kau nah ween Anishinaubaek k'dauh auwisseemim, gautawaenimaudjik aen-nigauzinidjin.

"Ahow!" Naudimoowaudauh k'bimigaedauguninaun noongoom" kitto meeniwauh baezhig zhushigauh. Ahow! Nana'b'oozoo k'gah k'weendumaukoh ae-izhi-tchigaeyaung geegoohnkaeyaung. Aubidaek k'gah izhi-itchigae meeyoow'ae-izhi-kik-inoomaudidumaukooyin.

Maudjeedoon gaenoowaubeeguk subaup, maudjeesh gayae k'kawiss woodih wauh dazhi geegoohnkaeyin. K'gah tikobinauh dush ae-iquayaubeeguk subaup mee dush tchi neesaubeeginut. Dah abi-ikoon dush geegoohnun. Apee baeshoowitaugoot k'kawiss w'dah nawudi-naun, w'dauh mindj-mauk-binaut k'aendumoonit tchi iko-waubeeginut.

"Gino-weendumauh goshah" kittoh Nana'b'oozoo.

Kego zaum chaunimaenimaukaen k'kawiss, kauween gaego dah izhi-waebuzissee. Keeshpin nindo-waenimutowauh nissiwih kemauh neewin kauween dush nawutch neebinuh. Keeshpin dush noondaesaeyin abi-waubung w'dah ayauwuk, mee igoh naussaub gae izheenoowaut.

Nana'b'oozoo gee waewaeb-quaenih, gee nissitootum. Mee dush w'gee ani-akeewaet wee awo-naunaut kawissun, subaup gayae. W'cheemauning Nana'b'oozoo w'gee gawaupeeginaun geegoohnmun, w'gee neesaubeeginaun kawissun. Mee igoh naussaub gauh izhi-waebuk meeniwauh w'gee mino-waungozih Nana'b'oozoo ae-apeet-chi-mino-waunig-aendung. Nana'b'ooboo w'gee winaendaun kissi-naunik, w'gee winaendung gauh izhi-aungaum-mikoot Zhushigaun; w'gee winaenimaun kawissun. Ae-apeet ishininit aetah geegoohnun w'gauh onushkawaekoot.

Nana'b'oozoo kawissun w'gee ani cheebyi-dauk-kaudaewidjih, mee igoh gayae ani-chauginigaet, wee gawautaut. W'gauh mook-ipeet "N'chauginigae, nosse w'd'inaun osse-un; kauween keeyaubih gaego gae meeninaumbaun; dae-minik geegoohnuk k'dayauwaumi-naudoog."

Gawaetaunih ae-izhi-netau-geegoohnkaeying, n'kawiss. Kauween maemikautch k'gah geegoohnseemim dazhi ningo geezis minik geegoohnuk ae-ayauwung! Onishishin washamae neebinuh w'gee nissung geegoohnuk."

"Ahneesh gae izhi-akeewaewinung geegoohnuk?" kawissun gagaewaedjimikoon.

"Mundjih eedoog. Kauween ganagae n'gee mukwo-aenduzee."

"Kauween nah k'dauh ningunausseemim omaum-apee tchi naunung k'd'oodaubauminaun. Kauween awiyah w'dauh baum-aenimausseen."

"Gaegaet suh nauh k'nebawaukauh."

"W'gee ani-akeewaewaut."

W'gauh dagooshinoowaut, kiweewizhaezhnish w'gee peendi-gae-puto "Oh! Ningushih! Gaegaet n'osse w'ge mino-waubumaewizih, minik geegoohnuk gauh daebinungidoowauh ae-apeetishinoowaut, aubidaek n'wee anookauzoomim doobaugun.

"Ahneen gauh ondjih beenaussee-gawaek neezh goonamauh maukawaenim!"

Kauween gaego meenwauh w'gee kittoossee, Nana'b'oozoo w'd'quaemun.

Apee w'gauh dittumoowaut geegoohnkauning kauween awiyah geegoohnun w'gee mukwowausseewaun mee igoh aetah shushi-waedjeeyaugin kotoowaunun.

"Ahneen! Aundih apeesh geegoohnuk. Nana'b'oozoo quae w'gee weesi-kawaewidum.

Tibee-ecdoog!"

"Gaegaet n'ningushih! Mee igoh omauh w'ningunigidoowaubun. Neen, n'gee daebinauk, n'gee abeedumoowauh dush n'osse, w'gee kooshimaun, n'gee waubumauh. Gonamauh zaum neebinuh gauh daebinauwingaen gauh izhi-aungawaummigoyaung. Kauween zaum neebinuh bizindausseen, washamae kiki-aendaussoh.

Awiyah w'gee noondoowauwaun gagaund-aupinit maegayauk, aenigook weeskawae-widumoon.

"Pukawiss!" Nana'b'oozoo gee zauzau-keewae, ningoting k'gah daebinin.

NANA'B'OOZOO – THE BEGINNING

The moment that the midwife placed Nana'b'oozoo in his mother's arms, he looked into her eyes and said, "My name is Nana' b'oozoo."

So startled was Winonah that she fainted. The midwife caught the baby before it fell to the ground. Nookoomiss gasped, "Eeeeyooh," as her knees buckled. "What kind of being have you brought into our world this time?" she asked. She watched her grandson and waited for him to say something more. But he said not a word. She spoke to her grandson to get him to say a word but he remained as if deaf and dumb.

That same day Nana'b'oozoo was born, word was spread that a newly born baby could talk, that he had told his mother that his name was Nana'b'oozoo.

"Aayaash!" people said.

"But Nookoomis heard him, and she doesn't lie."

"The midwife also heard him."

Of course no one would believe them. People scoffed. Whoever heard of a child talk the moment after he has taken his first breath?

Nana'b'oozoo didn't speak again until he was close to two and a half.

Not all people were skeptical of the story.

It was an extraordinary thing for a human being to talk at birth. Did not Winonah give birth to three extraordinary beings already? Could she not give birth to more?

There was something else unusual about Nana'b'oozoo. He was timid – as timid as a sparrow, a squirrel.

Not long after his birth, Nana'b'oozoo's mother died. Care for the baby fell upon the shoulders of old Nookoomiss.

What was she to do? Neighbours came to her aid, offered her what comfort they could and helped the little baby get over his anxieties. Once he got to know the insects, birds, animals, and what made the noises in the forest in the night, Nana'b'oozoo overcame some of his timidity, but not all of it.

When Nana'b'oozoo was six years old he asked his grandmother where his father and his mother were.

"They left," she said.

"Ooh?" was all Nana'b'oozoo said.

But someday he would want to know more.

To get his mind off his mother and father, Nookoomiss mentioned that Nana'b'oozoo would soon be of age to seek his vision. He should make preparations, now or soon, to make himself worthy to live a good life.

"What was the good life?" Nanan'b'oozoo asked.

"Ask the old men," Nookoomiss told her grandson.

Nana'b'oozoo rehearsed by day in the forests. At first exciting, the excitement soon wore off and became boring. The time for his vision came sooner than expected. Nana'b'oozoo wasn't ready.

Nookoomiss caught Nana'b'oozoo unready when she said, "It's time for you to go on an overnight fast." Nana'b'oozoo shivered and quivered in panic. He wasn't ready. He stammered and mumbled, "I'm not feeling well."

"Are you afraid?" Nookoomiss asked.

"No," Nana'b'oozoo answered weakly.

"Well then, get you going. I'm not asking you to go for several days, or out in the rain or far away. I'll keep you within hearing. Go! I'll tell you when to stop."

Nana'b'oozoo's knees nearly gave way as he drew away from his grandmother's side in the direction of the woods where lurked dangerous snakes and spirits, and spiders just waiting for him. He had gone no more than 75 paces when he stopped and asked his grandmother, "Is this far enough?"

"Go farther still! I can still see you."

Nanab'oozoo stumbled a few more steps before he halted once more to ask, "Is this far enough?"

"I can still see you... keep going until you're no longer in sight. Go on!"

Once more Nana'b'oozoo plodded deeper into the woods, tripping over stumps and roots, scratching his arms and legs on branches and rocks and other humps. At last he stepped into a hollow, lost his balance, and fell down. From where he lay Nana'b'oozoo couldn't see his grandmother and she couldn't see him.

"Is this far enough?" he asked, turning his head in the other direction and lowering his voice.

"I guess ... I can't see you. Stay where you are!"

"Okay Grandma!"

He said "Okay," but he did not mean it. He was scared. As soon as the glare of the fire went out, Nana'b'oozoo set out on his knees to go back as near as he could to their weegwaum.

Before the sun came up over the hills and brought morning, Nana'b'oozoo crawled back to the hollow where he had spent the night. Promptly, he fell asleep. He didn't wake up until his grandmother woke him later.

"Come! Wake up. You can't sleep all the winter, like a bear. You must be hungry. Poor boy," Nookoomiss said. "You must be tired."

Some months later Nookoomiss reminded her grandson that he was to seek a vision, as all men were to seek their vision until they had found it.

"I did go out," Nanan'b'oozoo argued, "but I didn't dream anything."

"I know," Nookoomiss said.

"How do you?" Nana'b'oozoo wanted to know.

"A bird told me that you didn't sleep; your belly told me that you needed food. Your spirit and heart need the dreams, and visions, and friendship of the manitous in order for your spirit to fulfill itself. So you had better do what you need to do to gain the friendship of the manitous and the spirits."

Nana'b'oozoo, now older and more eager to gain the good will of the manitous and gain their friendship, went to the holy places to be close to them. In one of his visits to their sacred sites, "Nana'b'oozoo kept his fast for two days," it is said. But deer came by his dreaming place and stirred up his hunger. He could not deny what his belly wanted and needed. Nanan'b'oozoo killed one of the deer and then ate until he could eat no more. Then he went to sleep.

"Did you dream?" Nookoomiss asked him the moment that Nana'b'oozoo stepped into the weegwam. What Nana'b'oozoo had was not an ordinary dream but a nightmare with bears and eagles, wolves, and turtles and thunderbirds that came and brought him blessings and favours.

"I hope you're telling the truth," said Nookoomiss.

NANA'B'OOZOO AUZHIDAE-WAUWAETAUGAE

Kabae-abi-boon Nana'b'oozoo w'gee boodoowaudaun w'd'mathi-nawaeziwin. W'dauh gee autae weenigoh keeshpin Nana'b'oozoo baubaumaendizigobunaen. Kauween dush w'gee boontoosseen Ween myeengun w'dindoowin. W'gee maenishigoon, w'gee maunikaugoon, goopitizit tchi inaenimikoot w'bim-gaedaugunun tchi daesidoo-waenimikoot, nawatch myeegunun kiki-aenduminit wauh izhi-bi-meek-audizoonit ween dush. Ay-aund datching w'gauh mukwo-aendung oshki-nitam w'gee nakawaeshkidaudiwaut, w'gee nissau-waut, oshki-ni-taugaewaut Kauween w'dauh winaenduzeen. Ondjitah! Aubidaek igoh gee weesigtoo aundjih meeniwauh tchi mashko-waendung wee auzhidae wauwaetoowaut myeengunun tchi mino-wauzit, Datching gauh mukwo-aendung wauh doodoowaut myeengunun Nana'b'oozoo gee gauskaus-aupih, w'gee moozhig-aendum gayae. W'gee mino-pidaun wauh doodung.

Naunaugata-waendun, n'daebawaenimikidoog myeengunish kauween gaego kikaendizeewaun, kauween Nana'b'oozoo w'kik-aenduzeen minik gae kiki-aendumoowaut needjaunisuk. Ahneen gae-ishi-bimeek-audizoot nishikaewizit maegawauk. Wausuh ishkawaeyaung abi-ayauh, baeskauh. Ahneesh gae-izhi diminae-waupun gaezheekaunit waesseehnun?

Nana'b'oozoo gee mino-abi-boonishih. Myeengauhsuk w'gee mino-waunigooziwuk, geewiniziwaut, weeki-bidoowaut zoowau-nugoomiwaun tchi matchi-dayae-ishininit, beenish w'gee naning dayaeshkaut nindoodjeenung zoowaunigooshun. Meekindji-ind kauween gaego inaenduzee, w'pakadaet maemidigae w'gee zinugikoon. Myeengunuk w'gee ningudiziwuk w'bim-ossaewaut, netaugawaut ween dush Nana'b'oozoo kaewih pakadae, aubidaek tchi weesinit ween, kauween maumidauh ween tchi babauminaund-ungibun tibishko myeengun Gonamah, ningoting dauh ani-nigudizih tchi kitchi-weesinit ningoting aen-dasso-neezhiwausso-geezhiguk. Chibwauh dittung maundah kishki-aewiziwin Nana' b'oozoo w'gee babaumiwidoon kunnish gauh cheecheegoondung apee gauh noogishkauwaut ningoodjih, mee dush gee geezhi-aukin-igaet kauween meeniwauh tchi weedjeewausseek myeenun meeni-wauh abi-booninik.

Mee auzhigawoh wauh-oozoosuk gee pidungeewaut, w'kiki-aendumoowaut baeshoowutinik zeegiwung. Goon gee maudjeenin-gizoh, metigook gee zeeginigaewaut, neebinaehnsiwuk w'gee piskau-beewaut mee gayae gee maudum-auzoowaut admoo wauwaut Gauh Abi-Boonikaehn.

Nana'b'oozoo weedjeewaugunun gayae w'gee dittaunauwauh mishi zeebi, mukwom auzhigawoh bauskaubun, Myeengun w'gee dautigi-quaenih gaego izhi-maundjigae, naussaub gauh doodu-moowaupun myeengauhnsuk apee gauh maegiwaushkidaudiwaupun.

"Waeginaen! Gaego nah k'dazhi-maundjigae?"

"Wauwaushkiwuk! Agauming" kittoh wyeengun.

"Ahneen gae izhi-tikumeeying!" oshki-neegishug gee nindo-ki-ki-aendumook.

"N'weedji-Anishinaubaek, aunindigoh, w'gee auzhi-waeshinook" w'd'inaun Nanan'b'oozoo.

"Gaegaet nah?"

"Aehn!" Nana'b'oozoo kittoh gagawaetaunih ae-apeetis-aenik w'd'inaendumoowin. W'dauh wae-izhaun myeengunun tchi-piko-apeesaenit." Mee suh gauh doodumoowaupun n'bim-gaedaugunuk. Chiwauh tikum-audigauwaut w'gee geeshk-awauwaun oshkig-inau-tikobhnsun maegawautch medaussiwih ashi nauno-dasso ozid ae-iquakozit. Apee gauh wizhteewaut w'gee tikumeewaut w'gee tikumaukishimauwaun oshkiginautikoon tibaewa-mukwoomeeng gayae; gauh mashkoowishking owih mukoomeen mee owih ininih w'gee boozidaubaunaut auzhigunautikoon w'gae tikumauk-ishi-maut meeniwauh neegaun wauh ani-izhaut aunikaeshimaut auzhi-gunautikoomun meeniwauh baezhig mukoomeeng, aeshkum w'gee baeshowitoon agauming, mee iko w'gauh izhih auzhiwaewaut, k'nissitootaum nah?

"Neen nitam n'gah tikumee" w'kittoh baezhig myeeng-auhn-zhish" Neen nitam, Neen nitam "w'kittowuk weekaunaehnun aupi-tchih igoh nauh nawautoowuk, beetoosh yoomb-gawaushkiniwuk, gaweek-kawaeshkawaewidumook.

"Kauween! Zaumneezaunut? Zaum k'gauhnsheehn. Neen? Nitam neen n'gah mitameegae."

Kakinah aen-datchiwaut w'gee nindo-waubundaunauwauh oshkiginautik maeno (de-mino) ginowaukizinit. W'gauh mukoowau-waut Nana'b'oozoo w'gee kiki-inoomoowaun myeengunun wauh izhi meeyau-gaubowiwaut, meeyauwi-ossaewaut wauuwiyae-idjee-aunik oshkiginautik. Nauning ditching myeenguniquae w'gee week-itchitoonaudoog tchi auzhidaewauwaet nawutch baeshau-bugoh, anootchizhi-kaudaesaet, kauween dush bunu-kummeesee. Myeeng-auhnsuk w'gee gino-waubumauwaun w'gushiwaun, tikumeenit zhooshkisdenit, zau-sau-keewaeniwaut apee dittuminit.

Chibwauh naukshininik w'gee muko-wauwaun noominaut-ikoon maeno-iniginoodjin. Aeni-waubung myeengun neebiwih agidjih noominautikoong. Nana'b'oozoo w'gee niminauwaenaun iniw noomin-autigoon wauuwiziwun, mee suh w'gee gaukook goondee, anootch izhi-kaudaenae myeengunish tchi bawauh piko-ipeesaet.

Aupitawa-eeng (aupita-gaum) myeengunish w'gee zhooshkishin, gauh soosawae-peeaussing nipeesh apee gauh pikitae-yaubeeshi-moot, gee ani-goondauwingoot. Myeengauhnsuk w'gee naneeniwi-daemoowuk w'gauh apeetchih gagaunisug-aendumoowaut.

"Kegoh gaego inaendungaegoon" Nana'b'oozoo w'd'inaun myeengauhnsun, Anishauh doodum k'gushiwauh, k'wee nindo wiyaezhimikoonaun, gauzoh auzhiwae mukoomeeng Kauween dush neen n'geewaut-sugoossee.

W'gee nindo-waewaemauwaun, beebaugimauwaun Nanawautch! Nanawautch. Nana'b'oozoo w'gee matchi-nawae-ikoon myeengunun doodaukoowaut.

Kegoh ningotchi izhaukegoon! Mee igoh zhae abeewishik Nindo-waewaemik, k'gushiwauh! Neen dush n'gah neesauwidjiwae, n'gah nakawae-igae negae-waussah. Ayau-apeetchin w'gee beebaug-imaun myeengunun "neetauwiss1"

Kauween dush awiyah w'gee nakawaetaukooseen aundjih gee ani-maunaudji-auh. Ani-apeesikaut w'nishkaudiziwin w'gee ani-aundji-ayaunih, chauenimaewiziwin, mee gayae nisitotaugoozit.

Awiyah geebeebaugimikoon "Waenaen baebau-nindo-waubumaut."

"Myeengun!" kittoh Nana'b'oozoo.

W'gae niboh, w'gee gabo-naubauwae. Apee w'gauh piko-peesaet Mishi-bizheu gee maudjee boonaun anaum-ipeeng, Kauween weekauh w'd'aub-cheeby-aussee.

Nana'b'oozoo w'gee geeshk-igidauzo. Ae-apeet-goondaugung tchi noondaugoot kakinah "Neen anaumeending n'gah izhauh. N'gah mawinaewauh. Apee gauh geezhi-uk kauween meeniwauh w'd'naesaesee." Mee dush w'gee maudidaemoot.

NEVER TAKE MORE THAN...

Our ancestors were fond of saying: "Don't take more than you need. There is more than enough for everybody, more than enough. If some people don't have enough it is because they didn't put enough effort in their labours. There is no need for people to be poor, there is so much abundance in the forests, meadows, lakes, rivers, skies. All men have to do is to imitate the ants and the bees in gathering the nectars of flowers and in keeping their homes well stocked with food. If some people are poor it is because they are lazy. No ants or bees are lazy."

Despite all the birds, animals, fish, vegetables, and fruit that grew and wandered about in the meadows and woods, soared about in the skies or swam in the waters, Nanan'b'oozoo and his family were often short of food.

Having little to cook and to feed her children made Nana'b'oozoo's wife quarrelsome. She nagged her husband.

"Why aren't you out there with other hunters tracking down deer or down at the lake getting fish? Must we always eat squirrels, groundhogs, skunks, and partridges?"

Their children often whimpered, "Daddy! Why do other hunters get more deer than you? Are they better hunters?"

Neither he nor she dared answer that question. Nanan'b'oozoo went out in a huff.

Down at the lake, Nana'b'oozoo saw a heron fishing. He made fishing look easy, as if there was nothing to it. How could the heron do the same thing every day? How could they eat fish every day?

The cold made Nana'b'oozoo forget the bland diet of fish three times a day, every day. He wished that he had worked as hard as his wife had wished him to work the past summer. Now, he would not be shivering and hungry, looking on.

"Ahnee!" he greeted the heron. "Would you help me? I'm not catching any fish. It may be my bait. What should I use?"

The herons argued amongst themselves whether they should show Nana'b'oozoo how to catch fish their way, the heron way, or leave him be.

"Let him suffer. He brings bad luck on himself," a few said.

"But it's the children that we must think of. They shouldn't suffer because of their father's follies."

"He doesn't listen!" some said. "He's lazy. He doesn't deserve any kind of help!"

Another heron agreed: "If it was only Nana'b'oozoo, I wouldn't help him one bit. Let him help himself. But let us help the children. Are we not supposed to be 'Good People' caring for others?

"Then let's help our neighbours this one time," said another heron who then yelled at Nana'b'oozoo, "but you must do exactly as you're told. Get a good long rope. After you have the rope, take your son with you to the place where you're going to fish. Tie him to the end of the rope and then let him down. A fish will come to him. When a fish comes near him, your son will seize him and tie him to the rope, and signal you to haul him in."

"But it's deep!" said Nana'b'oozoo.

"Don't worry about your son going under water, don't worry. Nothing will happen to him. If you need three trout take them but not more. They'll be there tomorrow."

Nana'b'oozoo nodded understanding. Then he went home to fetch his son and brought back a length of rope. In his canoe Nana'b'oozoo paddled his son to the fishing place. No sooner had he let his son down when the rope jerked. Nana'b'oozoo drew up his fish and let his son down once more. The same thing happened again and again. It was fun. He forgot that it was cold; he forgot the heron's warning; he forgot his son. He could only keep his eyes and his mind on the pile of fish he had thrown behind him.

Nana'b'oozoo's son couldn't feel his legs anymore and he was tiring. When he came back up to the surface he gasped, "I'm done, Dad! I can't do any more. We must have enough."

"Yes son, we must have more than enough. Yes, it's time to turn in, it's getting cold."

"But how are we going to get the fish home?"

"Never entered my head," said Nana'b'oozoo scratching his head.

"Can't we just leave them here? Go get our toboggan at home. Nobody'll bother them."

"Good idea, let's do that!"

"Oh Mom!" the son gasped as soon as he and his dad got in the door of their home. "Dad got so many fish today, a pile. We couldn't count them, couldn't even carry them home. We need a toboggan."

"Why didn't you bring two or three home with you so we could eat now?"

"Cut the talk, wife! You're coming with me! You're going to be proud of me!"

There was no answer from Nana'b'oozooquae other than a grunt. "Huh!"

When they got to the fishing grounds with their toboggan, Nana'b'oozoo and his wife found no fish, just blocks of ice in the shape of fish.

"Well! Where are the fish!" his wife shrieked.

"Who knows?" Nana'b'oozoo cried.

"But they were right there Mom! I caught them and I brought them to him. He put them in a pile. Honest! Maybe he caught too many. He was to catch no more than he needed."

"Ah! Your father will never listen," Nana'b'oozoo's wife screeched.

In the near woods there was derisive laughter.

Back and forth to the narrows Nana'b'oozoo went, each time drawing a longer trail of youngsters than before, carrying fish and doing all kinds of useful errands.

"What are you doing?" neighbours asked Nana'b'oozoo. "Expecting a famine? We've never seen you work so hard before! Haw, ha! Hah."

Up in the trees perched ravens, crows, buzzards, hawks, and jays clacking their beaks. Higher overhead swirled and swooped other birds waiting for a hand out; further back were squirrels and raccoons waiting for the fishers to let up their watch so that they could move in and help themselves. Some of Nana'b'oozoo's help volunteered to stay over for the night to keep freeloaders from helping themselves to free fish.

The sun set, its light set. Nana'b'oozoo grew weaker. Nookoomiss' arms and hands felt as if they were going to fall off.

"Don't you think that we have enough?" Nookoomiss asked. "I can't do anymore. I'm tired."

"I think – believe that we have enough fish to keep us without having to work for a while. You can sleep in Noko. You won't have to yell at me tomorrow morning. I'm so tired." He said no more. He stumbled home into bed and sleep without eating.

Nookoomiss was just as tired. Her eyes closed just as she stepped into her weegwaum; she crawled the rest of her way to bed.

As the night wore on the little guards fell asleep at their posts and the poachers, foxes, raccoons, skunks, hawks, ravens, and mice stuffed themselves all night. In the morning there were no fish.

MAUDJEE-KAWISS

Zhaungissiwih dasso-geezis gauh aundji-igiwigoot manitoun Ae-pungishmook, Winonah w'gee neegi-auwissoh, akiweewizaehnsun w'gauh izhi-inikaunaudjin "Kawiss."

Bidjeenuk gauh ondaudizinit abi-anoodjeehnsun, "kawiss" Ae-pungishimook w'gee abi-izhau abi-nindo-kiki-aenimaut waenaen dano-oon ininiwn w'gauh ossiwi-auniganaen apee nitau-iginit wauh auwunigawaen. Maegawauh beewoot (baubeewoot) Ae-pungishi-moot, w'gee inaubundumaun w'kawissun tchi netau-geewi-ossaenit, tchi mooshkinaenik sundjigonim tchi aumoowaut k'zheengaendau-guninaunik. Pekaun gayae ween Winonah gee inaubundakawae-moowaut kawissiwaun, tchi-mino-waubumaewizinit dazhi geewi-ossaet, kauween tchi minisinosseek babau-nindo-binikaet wee nissaut weedji bimaudizeen, ween gonamauh tchi maukinind kemauk tchi nitchigauzoot kauween weekwauk tchi kishki-aewizisseek tchi gautawaenimit ani-neenimiziyaun."

Auzhigoh gauh bim-ossaet Kawiss, w'ossun w'gee meenikoon metigwaub, pigookoohnse, pugumaugun gayae gae anook-auzoot, duminoot, kiki-noowautchi-itchigaet bimoojigaewin, waebitau-gaewin. Chibwauh neezhiwausi-abi-boonigizit, Kawiss washamae gee mitchaubaewizih, gazheekau, mashkawizee igiw dush waega-waen ininiwuk dazhi-odaenauh-akeeng. W'gee maumikaud-aendau-goozih. Aeshkum w'gee ani-weekishkautoowaun, baeshoowitoowaun ossun, aeshkum kabae-eeng w'gee ani-weedjee-auwaun ossun iniw dush gushiwun, gauh izhi-chaunim-aendumi-aut, ahneen ae-izhi

ayaumgaen; "apeetchin" w'kittoh Winonah N'chiboom, N'chechau-
koom, N'd'odaemah k'weedjeewikoot tibi-eedoog ae-izhauwanaen,
n'd'kiki-nawaezhiwinikoot tchi zhaubishkaumun nayauzaunuk gaego
tehi-izhi-waebuziseeyimbun.

Maegawautch medaussiwih ashi-nauno-dasso-abi-boon-gizis-
seebun Kawiss apee gauh maudjitaut miziwae-kummik babau-
maudizit maedaut-ishinaubaen w'd'akeemiwaung.

Ningoting ayae-oshkut w'gee mukooshkoowaun neegaunaubaen
geekitoonit. W'gee weekimikoon tchi bizind-audjigaet.

Mee nitam gee waubumaut geegitoo w-ininiwun pikidauk
goodaenik anikauwaung waubumaubeeyauk mazin-gawaudaenik
kiki-noo wautchitchigauhnsun. Ae-apeetaunikittooniwaut w'gee izhi-
inoowauwaun kik-noowautchi-itchigunun. Apeetchin awiyah w'gee
daebitaugozih "How! How?" Naussaub-aendung auskoowauwaut.
Kauween gee augoonaetawausseewaun gaugeegittoonit, w'gauh
apeetchi-mino-audjitoowaut kittoowinun, w'gauh apeetchi mino-
kizhae-audjitoowaut.

Maegawauh w'nawauwaut ae-ani-audijimoowausun Kawiss
w'gee gagawaedjimaun baezhig neegaunaubaen waenaen inaubiduk
iwih pikiduk-goodigun?

"Ooohn!" kittoh baezhik neegaunabae" waubamaubeeyauk
n'd'izhi-inikaudaumim-n'mukwo-waendumishkaugoonaum w'ae-
inaudjimoowinugiziyaung, w'gauh abi-zhaugooskumaung zaeniguk,
gauh dazhi-noondaeshinaung; gauh oondjeemiguk megoshae-mi-
naunind; ahneen ae-idumoowiniguk; ae-izhi-bae-baezhigoowaut
w'gee daeb-waewaendumook dibaendizoowaut, ogaukindaudizo-
owaut; n'mukwo-waendumikoonaun ae-izhi-daebinaeziyaung, ae-izhi-
dibitizatoowaungaeyiziyaung, w'ae-izhi nawuzhinae-maung tchi
naugudooying Anishi-naubae kiki-inoowaezhiwaewin tchi kiki-
aenimikooying mino-aenimung kakinah awiyah, kakinah gaego.
Datching gauh noondumaung wauh abi-naudiziyaung n'gee meek-
waenimaunik k'kitizeeminaunik, n'gee maenishizimin gayae. K'd'ayau-
naunaun nah gaego gae muko-waendumooninaek w'gauh abi-izhi-
waebuziyaek gauh abi-apeeskauyaek neegaunaubaek, w'gee gagawae-

dji'mauwaun Kawissun, w'gee ininimoowauwaun waumpum tibishko tchi daupinuminit.

Daebwaewaendung ininimaukoot tchi gagawaedj-idjeenung waeyaun Kawiss w'gee daes-inindjeenih tchi daupinung kiki-inoowae- zhiwaeyaun, apee w'gauh daunginung mee ae-queenoowaut ae-ayaudjik w'gee nissu-aenaumimauwaut "W'gee weeninaun waubumaubeeyauk! Nawadinik!"

"Maeno w'da'bimij-putoo!:

Ae-apeetchi kishko-nawaezit Kawiss, mee gee gaundissikummeet, ishkaeyaung w'gee ningunaun maedaut-ishinaubaen nindo-waewae- mikoot. "W'misqueeminih! Bim-audiziwinih!" Inawaewidumook.

Chibawauh wauh puwaet Kawiss gee noogi-putoo w'gee inauss- imi-gaubowitoowaut-baeminaushkaugidjin. Ningoting w'gee maudjee waebunung w'd'pugumaugunim mee igoh w'gee baushk-indibaewaut baeminaushkaukidjin. Apee aunind gauh noonduminit indib baus- kaunik w'gee noogi-putoowuk, mee dush gee geewitaushkoowau- waut Kawissun.

Kauween igoh waussuh ishkawaeyaung w'gee abi-ayausseewuk kaetizidjik "Kego nissaukaegoon! K'd'nawaendumaunaun. W'gee nissaun k'd'ogimauminaun. W'noondawauwaut w'kitizeewaun oonji- mikoowaut, minisinook w'gee oondjimeewuk. "W'gee nissaun goshah k'd'ogimauminaun. Kauween noongoom k'd'ayausseenaun gae neegaunish kaugiyaungibun!"

"Mee nee nauh iwih!" Mee dush meeyoow zaezeekizit gauh kittoot "K'nindo-waenimaunaun ogimauk gae kiki-inoowaezhiinaut minisinoon tibishko maubah ininih "mee dush ae-inaut Kawissun. "K'dauh mino-waudjimim keeshpin abi-weedjeeyaungishkinaun, Kawissinaun k'dauh izhi-daupinigoh. K'dauh inaendum nah tchi weed- ji-aki-waehnmiyaung, tchi neegaunaubidetoowatoowauk n'minisi- minonaunik" Kaetizidjik w'gee begoss-aenimauwaun Kawiss.

N'dauh mino-nawaendum tchi neegaunizeekindowigawauh k'd'minisinoowikoowauh. Aubidaek w'gee kiki-noowaudidaun aen- doodung w'dani-naudiziwin meenwauh tchi weendumoowaut gagawaedjimaut ossun tchi geekimigoot ahneen gae doodung.

Kakinah aen-datchiwaut gee mino-waubundaunauwauh w'ae-naukinigaet. Kawiss w'wee weendumoowaut w'neegee-ikoon w'bim-gaedaugunun, gawaek wee izhi-tchigaet. Maeshkoot Mukwo-nau-baek w'gee meenauwaun Kawissun – inaenimauwaun tchi kiki-noowaustchitoonit waubumaubeeyauk – tchi akeewaewidoonit, tchi akeewaewitumoowaut weedji-aki-waehnun.

Mee waubumaubeeyauk w'gauh ningutimaukiying Kawiss. Apee gushiwan w'neegi-aunit meeniwauh baezhig aki-weewiz-aehnsun w'gee aundji-inikaunauwaun Kawiss, nitam ozhaun, Maudjee-Kawiss w'gee izhi-nikauzoh. Owih dush oshki-abinoodjeehn "Kawiss" w'gee izhi-inkauzoh. Mee iwih apee k'kitizeeminaunik gee maudjitauwaut izhi-inikaunauwaut nitam-ozhaunun Maud-jee-Kawiss ondijih gee w'neegaun-ishkoowaut weekaunaehnun, kiki-inoowaezhiwaewaut, gautawaenimaut.

Maudjee-Kawiss gee kiki-inoowauziwaugunitoonun doodu-moowinun, kishkiyaewiziwinun, bawaudjigaewinun, gautawaendji-gaewinun, inaudjimoowinugiziwin, kiki-nawautchigun, waedauss-aewin.

WOLVES TEACH NANA'B'OOZOO

Nana'b'oozoo left his village and set out into the world. It was late fall when Nana'b'oozoo set out on his own leaving Nookoomiss to the care of her neighbours and to his other brothers. He had never been on his own before.

Not having been on his own before, Nana'b'oozoo didn't know where to pitch his camp. He set his little tepee in a beautiful hardwood bush with a lot of maple trees and lot of room between the trees for the winds.

The wind began to blow and the snow began to fall. Nana'b'oozoo looked about for kindling and firewood but there was none to be seen.

Just about this time a family of wolves, led by the mother, came along. The wolves were curious about the man. They'd heard about them but this was the first one they'd seen. They were not afraid of him.

"Who are you?" the mother wolf asked.

"I'm Nana'b'oozoo," said he.

"With a storm a brewing, you should be camping in a more sheltered spot in the forest," Mother Wolf said. Then turning to her offspring she added, "We'll keep Grandfather company and warm in case he gets cold during the coming night." The wolves curled up in little balls at Nanan'b'oozoo's feet. As they had expected Nana'b'oozoo began to shiver from the cold. The cubs moved closer and put their tails over him to keep him warm. Almost at once, Nana'b'oozoo was breathing heavily, snoring.

Not long after he was twisting and turning and flinging his arms out to throw off the cubs' tails. At the same time, he was gasping and coughing. He was too hot. "Phew!" he blew out. "Why didn't you wash? Your tails smell! They stink as if you dragged them through moose manure. I'll smell like a poop myself." But no sooner had he flung the tails off than he started shivering anew. He pulled the stinking tails back over him.

In the morning the pack and Nana'b'oozoo plowed through the snow drifts toward the evergreen forests. They pushed on until they all stopped, tilted their noses up in the air and took in deep drafts of deer scent that wafted in the wind.

"Why are you doing that?" Nana'b'oozoo asked. "Smell something?"

"Yes we do. We smell deer. A meal we're going to eat before the end of the day. Don't you smell anything?"

"Nothing!" was all that Nana'b'oozoo could say. To smell nothing made him feel ashamed. An animal could out smell him.

"Now boys," said Mother Wolf, "control yourselves, not too much noise, take your time. Look back at me from time to time. Remember that deer can smell and hear too. And knowing that we're in the neighbourhood makes them nervous. They don't know exactly where we are. Being anxious tires them out. The longer they are anxious the more tired they will be. You will save your strength and energy because you're going to need it!"

The boys went on ahead breaking a trail for their mother and Nana'b'oozoo.

"Alright boys," Mother hissed when she noticed her sons' tongues hanging out, "time for a rest."

The cubs lay down on the snow, panting. Nana'b'oozoo could not have gone further. He was done in too. He lay down some distance behind the cubs, beyond the hearing of the cubs.

"Well, my friend, which one of my cubs do you think is the best hunter?"

After a long look as if he had a good eye for good hunters,

Nana'b'oozoo said, "That one," pointing to a sleek, long tailed, agile cub.

"No, my friend," said the Mother Wolf. "Not yet; by and by he will be, right now he is too impulsive, wants to charge a buck without thinking. A buck would make short work of him with his horns. Try another one."

Nana'b'oozoo took a second look at the pack of cubs in front. "I would say the big one."

"No," said the Mother Wolf. "He depends too much on his size and his strength. With his speed and horns a buck would make that wolf look silly. Try again."

Three times more Nana'b'oozoo tried, three times more he couldn't guess right. "That one?" he asked not believing that a scruffy looking little wolf cub could be a good hunter.

"Yes, that one!" the mother wolf said.

"How could he outdo his stronger, quicker, faster brothers?"

"Just wait till we come to a herd of deer, then you'll see."

Nana'b'oozoo didn't say another word. He didn't know what to say. But he felt something in his heart. He felt as if the wolf looked down on him, as if he didn't know enough; as if wolf cubs knew more than he did, as if animals could teach humans. The thought that the wolf had a low regard for him nettled Nana'b'oozoo. He had pride, he was someone, and he had abilities. He could get back at the wolf. He would make the wolf look silly.

NANA'B'OOZOO NAWUTCH WEENGAEZIH

Aen-dasso-gizhaeb Nookoomiss w'gee nitcheewitoo "Tuguh winishkaun! Kishkoozin! Kaebae-geezhig nah k'wee nebauh? Kauween
nah gaego k'inaenduzee daessido-waenimikooying k'bimigaedau-
guninaunind, Gaegaet suh nauh kitimishkih owih Nana'b'oozo-
oozhih apaenimoondoowaut ookoomissun – ween, mee igoh aetah
dan-aukshing nebauguning, aupitchi w'mino-pidaun gaego anoon-
akeesik, nawaebit, kitimaudizih. Ningoting, apee maudjaunit ookoomissun mee kikaendung kitimaudiziwin. Noongoom zaugitoon kitimi-
iwin, w'zheengaendaun anookeewin; w'gee zaugitoon nebauwin
w'gee zaugikoon. Nana'b'oozoo w'gee zaugidizooh. Kaetizidjik w'gee
aungawaumimaun oshki-neegi-quaen "Kego baumaenimaukegoon
Nana'b'oozoo. Kaugigae kummik k'gah geesaudizim, k'gah baumi-
naundaum.

Aubiding Nana'b'oozoo gee nishkigoom ookoomissun beebau-
gumikoot. Winishkaun! Ahneesh minik datching gae weendumau-
koowinaen. Winishkaun! K'gageebishae nah?"

"Anookeen! Anookeen! Anookeen! Meenah aetah gae-kiki-
aendumun" Anookeen! "Mee nah aetah kae-kik-aendumoowaut
kaetizidjik. Mee tibishko ae-izhi-apeet-waewaendumaek nebauwin,
nawaebawin matchi-auwung.

Kauween izhi-onishishizeenoon ae-izhi-anoon-akeeying ae-izhi-
nawaebiying gae izhi onishishingobun weengae geezhaukini-
gaewaupun, keeyaubih washamae dauh mino-kaugunaun, w'dauh
mino-ayauwuk washamae gae daneewaupun. Keeshpin Anishinau-

kaek geegoohnkaewaupun nigo-geezis gaetinaumiziwaupun gaegaet
dauh maumoowishimauwauh dae-minik geegoohnun, kauween
maemikautch w'dauh anookeesseewuk ningot neezhiwauss-gee-
zhig, Kauween maemikautch w'dauh nashkawaetautoosseewuk
aen-dassso-geezhiguk tchi awo naudji-meedjimaesseewauk tibishko
aen-doodumoowaut noongoom aen-dasso-geezhiguk.

"Kaween k'nissitotoosseenoon" w'd'ikoon ookoomissun.

"Nashkae!" w'd'inaun Nana'boozoo ookoomissun" K'gah kiki-
noowaudaudjimootoon, Keeshpin awo-geegoohn-kaeyaun aen-dasso-geezhiguk aenowaek neebinuk geegoohnuk n'dauh mauwaund-
jimauk kauween nah?"

"Gonamauh!"

Kauween K'dauh geekaundusseemim ondjih zaum-ingawaumi-
yaun, zaum weekauh kuhkooziyaun; kauween nah. Washamae w'dauh
onishishin weedookidaudiying, kauween nah?

"Ayauh! Aundih wauh dazhi ganawaenimungidoowauh geegoohnuk? Waenaenuk wauh piku-ozhauwaewaut geegoohnun waenaenuk
wauh bimeekungik sundjigoomin? Tibikuk? Geezhiguk? Mindimooyaehn izhi-aunoowitum? Baekauh w'gee naunaugizo-waubu-
maun ozhishaehnun geeshkoowaunit oshki-ginautikoon inaukshi-
maut wizhitoonit gauskitizigaun aundih gae dazhi gauskiziwaut,
bautaezoowaut geegoohnun, waesseehnun gayae. Nubunuh dasso-
igoon Nana'b'oozoo gee nindumeekae.

Ishkawautch Nana'b'oozoo bunu-goodoon zhimaugun gauh
dazhi geen-boodoot chibawauh minda-aupeet aen-dazhi geegoohnkaewaut Anishinaubaek, zheebaunauning Weebah w'gee abi-kee-
wae-daubaunaun medaussiwih ogaun.

"Waenaen wauk pika-ozhaunaut" gagawaedawae Nana'b'oozoo
ookoomissun.

"Keen suh."

"Eeeeeyooh! Izhi-geedawaemoh mindiwoomooyaehn "Kauween
nauh kishkitoossen kabae-geezhig tchi anoonakeeyaumbaun, n'dauh
gawi-nae chibawauh nauwi-quaek."

"Kego mashi-aunisheetungaen. N'gah weekumauk neesh, nissiwih, neewin mindimoohnaeyuk gae naudimaukiyin." W'gauh kittoot iwih Nana'b'oozoo w'gee maudjee-kunaeshing wee awo-nindo-in-aewaut mindimooyaehnun. Weebah w'gee auwun mee w'gee zaugaewaet, neewin mindimoozaehnun abi zigau-beeginaun tchi-abi-weedookoowaunit ookoomissun tchi bauboodawaewaut apee naunaun-koonaek, tchi pikuozhauwaewaut, tchi gauskizoowauwaut geegoohnun, ikoonauzhiwauwaut gimoodinauhnsun gayae. Auzhoog suh Nana'b'oozoo gee dano-ossaedoog zheebaunauning ae-indaut gayae. Datching gauh akeewaut, akee-oomaut geegoohnun nawutch gee mazheenoowun oshki-neegishun gauh noopinunigoodjin anootch gaego gauh dooduminit wee naudimaukoot auwidjwiinaut geegoohnun.

"Ahneen aen-anookeeyin?" gagawaedjimikoon bimigaedaugunun. "K'daeb-waewaendum nah wee minaeyauk meedjim, weeyauss, tchi dani-inaundumoowaut k'weedji-bimaudizeenaunik. Weekauh k'waubumisseenoon tchi kitchi-anookeeyin. Gaego k'kiki-aendau-naundoog! Weendumooshinaung! Ahneen wae-ondji gaudooyin?"

Iship-autikoong dan-ubiwuk kaukaugeehnuk, aundaegook, weenaungaek, kaikaikook, deendeehnsiwuk, medayaukoozhaeh-nook. Washamae keeyaubih ishpiming-baum-aushiwuk-bimaun-gaewuk benaewak baubeetoowaut ishkoondjigun tchi ningudji-au-daek. Negae-waussuh begoss-aubiwaut sunigook, aehnsibunuk, Wiyae-oshkut aupitchi igoh gaezhau-audigaedjik gee nawaud-jeewuk, gee mino-waeziwuk-zaubiziwuk. Kauween ginowaesh gee auwuhnzinoon mee gee aub-aenduzeenauwauh tchi iko waubu-waut, w'gee nushkiwaeziwuk.

Gee pungishimoh, mee gayae gee ani-tibikuk. Nana'b'oozoo gee ani-chaug-eewee. Nookoonus, tibishko wee kidiski-anikaesaet gee inumdjiwooh, wee kidis-inindjeet.

"Dae-minik nah k'd'ayaugauminaudoog" kitto mindimooyaehn "Mee igoh chauginigaeyaun, n'd'auno-waewiss.

Mee igoh gayae neen ae-izhi, ayaek-kunaeyaun Ningot geezis k'gah weesinimim k'd'ayauminaudoog geegoohnug, nissim dunnuh dasso-igoon kauween maemikautch k'gah anookeesseemim; mee aetah tchi cheebaukawaeying, weesiniying. Noko! K'dauh booz-ingawaumim, n'gah nebauh, Kauween maemikautch k'gah beebaugu-missee waubung gizhaeb. N'd'ayaekwus.

Naeneezh gee cheecheesh-ozidae-kummeewuk ae-ani-peendi-gaewaut. Mee aetah w'gee medaedjaunae ingawaumook.

Gauh ani-ishpi-tibikuk gaezhaunaupuneek geegoohnun geekeepun-goshiwuk mee gee ani-nebauwaut. Gauh ani-nebauwaut, mee gimood-inauhnsuk w'gee mookeewaut, waugooshuk, aehnsebunuk, zhigaugook, kaikaikook, kaugaukisheehnsheek, waesseehnuk, kayaushkook w'gee naudimaudizoowaut meedjim; wauweesiniwaut beenish gee goodaumiwaut kakinah gauh ataemigukibun. Kakinah w'gee meed-jiwaut. Kauween gaego gee ishkoosaesseenoon.

Gauh kishkoozit mindimoohnyaeh, goodjeeing w'gee izhauh, aya-naubit, nindo-waubumaut geegoohnoomiwaun Kauween awiyah, kauween gaego, kauween ganagae kunaehnse.

"Eeeeeyooh! Nana'b'oozoo" weeskawaewidum "Awiyah k'gee kitinimaukoonaunk'geegoohnminaun! Eeeeeyoooh!" K'daesid-awaeni-mauk k'bimgaedaugunaunik ae-izhi-bugwoonwiziwaut washamae keen, kiki-aendaun wauh izhi ningudjitooyin anookeewin Kauween wee mino-nawaed'awauh k'bim-gaedauguninaunik k'd'ondjih izhi-itchigaesee; keen tchi kishkitimaudizooyin nebauwin, nawaebiwin. Nashkae dush gauh doodaudizooyin.

CHEEBY-AUB-OOZOO

Winonah became a mother for the third time. She and Ae-pungishi-mook called their son Waub-oozoo. By the time that he was seven it was clear to the father that his son was not going to be a warrior or a master hunter. He was much too mild; he could not stand the sight of blood. He would never amount to anything. Unable to count on his son to serve his people, Ae-pungishimook went back to his rounds.

Waub-oozoo felt bad for not having pleased his father, but relieved that his father was gone from his life. No more would he get bawled out or punished for missing his mark, or crying for a wounded deer.

After his father had passed on, Waub-oozoo turned to his grandmother for comfort and learning. He wasn't afraid to ask her about manitous, spirits, souls; whether trees and flowers had spirits; whether deer, rabbits, mice, eagles, and fish had spirits. Where did spirits live? Did they listen to humans? Did they talk to men and women? What did they look like? Were they friendly or unfriendly?

Waub'oozoo's grandmother had a hard time answering the questions that her grandson put to her. Yes, there were spirits and souls. Men and women can't see them because they are invisible, but we know that every being and thing has one of each. When an arrow strikes the heart of a deer or a bear, the animal dies, the soul and the spirit are said to have gone from the body. The body can no longer see, hear, taste, feel, move, sense. There are good spirits, most of them are good – caring for someone, or something. Some live in the sky, some lie on earth in hard to-get-to places for humans:

caves, chasms, summits of mountains, whirlpools, rapids, giving these places a sacred, mystical aspect.

"I'd like to talk to them!" Waub-oozoo said.

"Leave them alone, Grandson. You might stir them up!"

Much as he wanted to please his grandmother, Waub-oozoo could not get the manitous or spirits out of his mind. As often as he could, Waub-oozoo went to those places where they were said to dwell. There, he spoke to the manitous as respectfully as he could, but Waub-oozoo went on to tell them that people were afraid of them. They didn't mean to trouble the spirits, people only wanted to know how to get along with their neighbours; what to do, what not to do.

But nary an answer did he receive form the spirits. They were there. Waub-oozoo knew they were there. He could sense them watching him, listening to him.

It was this knowing that they were wherever he was that kept Waub-oozoo from giving up the attempt to talk to the spirits.

One day, some years later, Waub-oozoo went out into the woods where there was a thick growth of ferns. There he fell asleep.

Weeng, the ogimauh of sleep, took Waub-oozoo to the Land of Dreams. In the dream the spirits showed Waub-oozoo how to make a drum and how to beat it rhythmically so that the echoes of the drumbeats carried the song through the skies to the dwelling places of the spirits. With the drum, men and women could get the attention of the spirits. But only men and women of good will got to hear what the spirits had to say.

On awakening, Waub-oozoo made a drum just like the one that the spirits had shown him how to make. He composed chants to carry his heart's feelings.

The people did not take up Waub-oozoo's habit of seeking talk with the spirits, of asking for guidance. It was only after they had noticed that some hunters killed more deer than other hunters or caught more fish than some of their neighbours.

"Luck, good luck," some said.

"It is Kitchi-Manitou that gives good luck to the grateful and withholds it from the ungrateful."

This was the explanation for the uneven granting of favours -- that some hunters had the good will and friendship of the spirits. The hunters who were frequently rewarded must have had a more powerful medicine in their prayers and in their hearts. It was as well a reward for the respect and honour paid by the hunter to the deer, or whatever had given its life for the hunter's health and for that of his family.

There were good and unfriendly manitous and spirits. There were Thunderbirds who keep Mother Earth refreshed and fertile; and there was the Great Lynx who kept the waters safe and clean. Ever at war, they sometimes killed people. Once, the Thunderbirds so overdid their irrigating the land that they flooded it and drowned humans and animals.

To prevent floods from covering the land ever again, Waub-oozoo showed our ancestors what to do. Upon hearing the rumbles of the thunders our elders offered tobacco and asked the Thunderbirds to be moderate in their release of water. Men and women were to 'walk in balance,' that is, to control their emotions and appetites, and make use of their 'common sense.' Once a year, a person was to go on a purification retreat in the forest. There, in a pool of water, he would look at his image. He'll ask himself, "Who are you?" Then ask them, "Who am I? What are their stories?"

Our ancestors looked on Waub-oozoo as a wise man, an upright man. He talked to the manitous who told him what to do, what to say, what he wanted to know. With the manitous as his advisors, men and women came to Waub-oozoo for counsel. His neighbours said, "Ask Waub-oozoo, he'll talk to the manitous, they tell him what should be done."

Waub-oozoo was young when people began coming to him for advice. It was then that he listened to his heart and married a 'good woman' who would 'tell him what to do.' All his brothers, Maud-jee-Kawiss, Pukawiss, Cheeby-aubooz, and Nana'b'oozoo were there.

At the outset the get-together was friendly but it soon turned nasty. It started with Maudjee-Kawiss making light of Waub-oozoo's habit of asking the manitous for their help in overcoming difficulties as they make their way of life – path of life. That is what the faint of heart do – call on the manitous to come to their aid.

Waub-oozoo was stung by these words. He got up from his place, went to his weegwaum. When he came out his face was painted black and red and he performed a brief war-dance. After this short act of war he took his canoe down from its resting place and carried it to the shore.

Guessing what Waub-oozoo meant to do, the neighbours, all of them, tried to talk him out of leaving then. "It's too rough now. It's going to get rougher still when the wind picks up even more! Wait till the wind dies down. You don't have to show that you're not a coward right now."

But nothing they said could talk Waub-oozoo from going through his plan to set out that night.

"Fool!" they said wagging their heads. They looked on in silence as Waub-oozoo battled with the waves to keep his craft afloat and direct into the wind. Up one wave, down another went Waub-oozoo, rising and falling with each wave until he paddled out of sight into the dusky murk.

Next morning an early riser came upon the wreckage of Waub-oozoo's canoe. He at once raised the hue and cry that brought the villagers to the shore. Among them came Nana'b'oozoo to the launching place. There he wailed in a loud voice calling out to his brother to come back to them and threatening the waters and Mishi-Bizheu to return their victim to life. "Come back! Come back!" he cried.

"Needjee! Not too loud, not too sad!" Nana'b'oozoo's neighbours reminded him. "Remember you'll sadden your brother's soul-spirit only more. Think of him as a great gift who tried to show us how to live in harmony with each other and how to walk in balance as we make our way along the path that we have chosen."

But the tender words and thoughts of his neighbours didn't temper Nana'b'oozoo's grief; it only made him cry harder. While the neighbours on shore were out looking over the waters, someone broke the surface of the waters. The crowd gasped. "A person from the underworld!" Nana'b'oozoo gave a loud cry and ran into the water to welcome his brother to the Land of the Living. Before he had taken too many steps, neighbours seized Waub-oozoo[7].

While the men who had caught Nana'b'oozoo struggled and shouted to settle him down, the rest waved their arms and yelled at his brother, "Go! You belong in the World of the Dead!" He was now Cheeby-aub-oozoo, chief ghost. "Stay away from our homes!" they told him.

Cheeby-aub-oozoo, their former neighbour, turned about, and, step by step, was swallowed back by the sea.

CHEEBY-AUB-OOZOO

Ae-ikonissing Winonah gauh neegi-auwissoot aki-weewizaehsun w'gee bimi-maudji-aun. Waub-oozoo gee izhin-ikaunauwaun. W'gauh neezhiwausso-abi-boonigizit. Mee gee kiki-aendaugizit kaween weekauh wee minisinohwissee, kauween weekauh wee nindo-waend-jigaessee. Zaum gee nookaudizih, gee mauzh-odae-ae-ishkaugoon misqui. Kauween weekauh dauh apeet-aendaugoozissee. Baewi-aenimaut kawissun Ae-pungishimook gee piskaubee aendazheepun.

Waub-oozoo w'gee maun-aendam gee matchi-nawae-aut ossun, w'gee nigunikoot. Kauween dush meeniwauh dauh nitcheewitchigaussissee kemauh dauh pizhuzhaegauzzoossee mawimaut wauwaushkaeshiwun.

W'gauh maudjaunit ossun Waub'oozoo w'gee izhaumaun w'ookoomissun tchi aungawaudjgoot, tchi gagawaedjimaut tchi weendumaukoot tchi kikinoowaud-audjimootaukoot ahneen ae-izhi-inaugooziwaut manitouk, chiboomuk, cheebyuk; aendoogawaen metigook, wauskoon wauwaushkaeshiwuk, wauboozook, wauwau-begoo-anoodjeehnsuk, migiziwuk chiboom-wiwaugawaen. Aundih gauh daniziwaut? Bizindowauwaun nah Anishinaubaen? Ginoonauwaun nah? Ahneen ae-izhi-inaugooziwaut? Neezauniziwuk nah? Mino-neewigiziwuk nah?

Ookoomiss gee zinugizih kikinoo-waudaudjimootoowaut ozhishaehnun. Aehn! Ayauwuk igoh cheebyuk, manitouk. Kauween Anishinaubaek waubumauseewaun, kauween inaugoozisseewuk; missowauh igoh kikaenimaunaun, kiki-aendaunaumim ayauwaut.

Apee pigook meekooshkaukoot wauwaushkaesh kemauh mukwoh, owih waesseeh niboh. Chiboomiwaen, cheebyiwaun maudjauwun, mee igoh ningudumoowat weeyoow. Mee aunoowaewut weeyoow tchi waubit, noondumaet, moozhung, kauween gaego kishki-aewiziwin. Baepekaun izhi-waebiziwuk manitouk, gauta-waendaunauwauh gaego, gauta-waenumauwaun awiyah. Aunind dasseewauk, aunind daneewak agid-kuminik, ningodjih igoh nauh waussuwae-kummik weembaubikauk, agidau-widjew, waeswicjaedjiwung, bauwitigawaewaeyauk, w'ae-ondjih zhawaendaugook, Manitouwaendaugook.

"N'dauh mino-waendum tchi-ginoonigaubun" kitto Nana'b'oozoo.

"Kegoh baumaenimaukaen! Ganamauh k'gah nishki-auk. W'gee nindo-waendaun tchi mino-nawae-aut ookoomissun kauween dush w'gee kishkitoosseen tchi winaenimaut manitoun, cheebyun. Aen-dasso-dawissaet Wau'b'oozoo w'gee izhau aundih aen-dazhi abeetuminit manitoun. W'gee ginoonaun, weendumoowaun zaegaendaugiziwaut, zaegauwaut Anishinaubaen. Kauween gee nindowaendizeenauwauh tchi megoshkaud-tchigaewaut wee nindo-kiki-aendaunauwauh aetah wauh izhi-mino-nawaendiwaut, weekaunaendiwaut. Ahneen gae doodumoowaut tchi mino-nawawaeyaut bimigaedauguniwaun?

Kauween weekauh gee nakawaetaukooseen manitoun. Gee ayauwak. Nana'b'oozoo gee kiki-aenimaun ayaunit baeshoh w'gee mozhi-aun gino-waubumukoot, bizindaukoot.

Kiki-aendung-maundah, kiki-animaut ayaunit cheegi-eehn gee zoongi-dae-aeshkaugoon, w'gee zheeb-aendum, daeb-waewaendum ningoting tchi ginoonigoot.

Aubiding, weekauh igoh nauh maundah Waub-oozoo gee chaekaukwoom aundih gauh dazhi zhingoobeekauk, Ayaekoozit mee omauh gee awoh nebaut.

Weeng, gauh ogimaukindung nebowin w'gee maudji-naun Waub'oozoon Pawaudjigae-kauning. Maegawauh nebaut Waub'oozoo gee abi-izhaumikoon manitoun gauh izhi-inoomaukoodjin wauh izhih medawaewae-igunikaet, wauh izhi daewae-igaet gawaek tchi buzawaewaesing geezhigoong, manitouwauning abeetemoowaut manitouk w'd'nawaendauguniwaun gayae. Anookauzoowaut meda-waewae-igunun, Anishinaubaek w'dah bizindaukoowaun manitoun.

Apee gauh kishkoozit Waub-oozoo w'gee wizhi-aun meda-waewae-gunun; gee ningumoonun animi-aewinun gauh oonjeen-igin odae-ing.

Kauween paubigae w'bim-gaedaugunun gee kiki-waubumauss-eewaun Wauboozoon ginoonaunit manitoun tchi geekimikoowaut. Mee paumauh gauh gaeski-waubumauwaut aunind bim-gaedau-guniwaun washamae neebinuh wauwaushkaeshiwun nissaunit, washamae neebinuh geegoohnun akeewaewinaunit. Ahneesh igoh nauh? Mino-waubumaewiziwaun gee meen audoog. Aunind gee izhi-waubundaunauwauh. Kizhae-manitou zhawaenimaun iniw meegawaetch-waenduminit; zaugitumoowaun iniw meegawaetch-waendumoosseenik. Mee dush maundah gauh izhi kiki-inoowau-didumoowaut Anishinaubaek, aunid nawutch mino-waubemaewizi-iwaut, weedj-aki-waehnmikoowaut manitoun. Ahneen iniwuk zhaewaendaugozidjik washamae onishishidoogaenuk. Beetoosh zhawaenimikoowaun waesseehnun ondji mino-audji-auwaut waes-seehnun gauh meenikoowaut weeyaussimih tchi ginaundiziwaut.

Dagoowuk manitouk, maumeeshook gayae. Animakee-ben-aessiwuk w'bimeekawauwaun mizu-kummik-quaen; been-aubau-wunawaut tchi netau-ozhaenit; mishi-bizheu gee gino baendaunun gummeen tchi been-augummik. Apeetchin dapinidoowaut gee pitchin-nauwaun Anishishinaubaen, Ningoting maegowauh nissaubau-wi-djigiwaut w'gee zaumaubauwidjigaewuk gee gaboonaubauwinau-waut Anishinaubaen, waesseehnun gayae.

Tehi zaum-tchigaesseeninik meenwauh Waub-oozoo gee kiki-inoomoowaun k'kitizeeminaubuneek gae doodumoowaut. Apee noondoowaut animikeen abeed waewiduminit w'dah pagidinu-moowauwaun saemaun, ae-izhi-gagaewaedjimauwaut tchi naegaut-chi-tchigaenit, tchi mino-nawae-auwaut manitoun, Anishinaubae-buneek dah meeyau-ossaewuk tchi naegautchitoowaut, aungiwaud-jidizoot tchi gaugeetau waendumoowaut, gaugeetauwizinaut.

Ningoting aen-dasso-abibooniguk w'dah awo-madootizoh baemau-dizit maegayauk, apeetchin w'dah gino-waubundiziwuk nipeekaung. Maezinautaeshing k'gah gagawaedjimauh. "Waenaesh keen? Neezhing, nissing k'gah gagawaedjimauh "Waenaesh keen?" K'gah gagawaed-jimik maeshkwoot "Waenaesh keen? Ahneen ae-inaudjimoowi-nukiziyin?"

K'kitizeeminaubuneek w'gee daeb-waewaenimauwaun Waub-oozoon gaugeetauwizinit, gawaek-waudizinit. W'gee ginoonaun, w'gee weendunaukoon gae doodung, gae kittoot, gae kiki-aendung. Geek-imikoot manitoun bimi-gaedaugunun w'gee abi-izhaumikoon tchi gawaek-ishimaut, tchi kiki-inoomoowaut. Baekaunizidjik gee kittoowuk gagawaedjimik Waub-oozoo. W'dak ginoonaun mani-toun gae weedumaukoot ahneen gae izhitchigaengibunaen.

Waub-oozoo oshki-neegeebun apee bimigaedaugunun gauh maudjitaunit abi-izhaumikoodjin. Mee maegawautch gauh weedi-gaet, weedigaemaut baezhig mino-quaen.

Kakinah Waub-oozoo weekaunaehnun, Maudjee-kawiss, Pukawiss, Nana'b'oozoo, ge abi-izhauwun.

Ayae-oshkut gee mino-waunig-waendumook nakawaeshkidau-diwaut. Kauween ginowaesh gee auwuhnzeenon mee gee geekaun-didiwaut. Maudjee-kawiss gauh maudjitaut naunaundikoomaut Waub-oozoon apaenimoondoowaunit manitoun tchi naudimau-koot tchi zhaugooskung gaego zaeniguk kemauh naeneezuk gae audaukishkaugoot, ae-ani-naugadoot bimaudizi-meekunnuh. Mee zheeyaug-odae-ae-aedjik aen-doodumoowaut apee naeneezaunuk maegawaushkumoowaut.

Waub-oozoo w'gee weesiginaeshkaugoon kittoowinun geebi-zigawcc, izhaut ae-indaut. W'gauh abi-zaug-ung w'gee makatae-waun-geengawae, ae-inaundaek misqui ae-kiki-inawauzi-inaundaek misqui bae-midjiwung meegaudiwining.

W'gee neemih, w'geezausau-keewae, w'gauh geezheetaut neemit w'gee naudin w'cheemaunim. Bimigaedauginimun dubub-aenimikoot wauh dooduminit gee ondjimauwaun "Kegoh! Ningodjihi zhaukaen. Zaum nitcheewut noongoom! Baubeetoon tchi boonuk! Nawutch wee gotaumigut. Baubeetoon tchi boon-aunimuk kauween maemi-kautch k'dauh waubundawaessee noongoom zhaugood-odae-aes-seewun.

"Geebautch!" aunind gee kittoowuk waewaeb-quaeniwaut. W'gee gino-waubumauwaun Waub-oozoo cheemaunim anim-koosing tibaewih. W'gee beebaugih tchi nindomaut bimigaedaugunun. Gee bigum-putoowuk, Nana'b'oozoo gayae omauh niminawaegunming mee dush omauh gauh dazhibeebaugumaut weekaunaehnun tchi abi-akeewaenit tchi aushimaunit nipeekaun mishi-bizheu "Abi-akee-waen! Abi-akeewaen!" inawaewidum.

"Needjee! Kegoh zaum gazheewaekaen! Kegoh zaum naneeni-wae-maukaen gauh maudjaut", w'bimigaedaugunun gee aunga-waem-mikoon. Mukwo-aenim kaetae-audizidjik gauh kittoowaupun. K'gah naetawaenimauh cheebyimun nawautch. Mukwo-aenim tibishko kitchi-meenikoowiziwin wauh weekitchitoot tchi kiki-in-oomaukiying wauh izhi-mino-nawae-kaundiying, meeniwauh gae-izhi-meeyauwi-ossaeying maegawauh naugudooying bim-au-dizi-meekun.

Kauween gaego gee naubutussineenih aungawaudjiming Nana' b'oozoo. Washamae gee gazheewae-daemoh. Maegawauh dab-au-bundjiwaut baezhig waegawaen-isheedoog gee mookipeeshkum. Kakinah awiyah gee noondaugiziwuk zaegikoowaut munisoohnun, "Eeeyooh! Cheebyh!" Nana'b'oozoo gayae gee noondaugozih mee dush gee gaundisi-kummeet wee piko-ipee-putoot, w'wee awo-na-kawaeshkoowaut weekaunaehnun.

Missowauh ae-apeetch-putoot kauween waussuh gee bigumeesee mee gee nawudinikoot bimigaedaugunun. W'gee kiki-aenimauwaun wauh dooduminit.

Maegawauh ininiwuk gee mindjmaukinauwaut, weendummowau-waut "Baekayaun!" Ogow aunind Anishinaubaek w'gee ikoonauzhi-wauwaun iniw Cheebyun. "Kego nawutch baesho abi-izhauken. Kauween keeyaubih k'dibaendaugozissee agid-kummik. Noongoom, cheebyi-akeeng k'dibaendaugooss. Keen k'ogimaukindaun chee-by-akeeng k'ogimaukindoowauk cheebiyuk. Kegoh, baumaenimishkingaegoon." W'gee noogi-gauboowih. Anishinaubaek w'gee wauwau-tikoomoowauwaut ningodjih tchi zhaunit.

Naegautch, baekauh cheeby-oozoo w'gee nauwug-quaenih tchi zhaunit.

Naegautch, baekauh cheeby-oozoo w'gee nawug-quaenih tibishko kishk-aendung ningunaut bim-igaedaugunun. Mee dush gee ani-maudjaut, w'gee goondauwigoot.

Gee ningudimauginaun medawaewaeginun, gae-izhi ginoonau-waut manitoun, tchi kiki-inawae-izhiwaenikoowaut mino-nawae-in-diwuning, tchi meeyoowi-ossaewaut, tchi nindo kiki-aendizoowaut midootizauning.

NANA'B'OOZOO'S REVENGE

All winter long Nana'b'oozoo nursed his ill will. It would have gone away by itself, if he had let it be, but he couldn't let it go. It was Wolf's fault for putting him to shame. She made him look dumb as if even wolf cubs knew and could teach him more about hunting and caring for himself than he could. Again and again he recalled the memory of the first time they met and the first time they got their first deer. He couldn't let the memory go. He needed to bring it back, to feel the hurt once again so that he, Nana'b'oozoo, could pay back Wolf, and have some fun out of it. Every time he thought of a trick that would make wolf look foolish, Nana'b'oozoo chuckled and his spirit cheered up.

In afterthought, Wolf was right; Nana'b'oozoo didn't know as much about hunting as her cubs did and he was a slow learner who needed to do a lot of catching up.

He had a good winter with the wolf pack. The cubs liked removing their tails from Nana'b'oozoo's back on real cold nights and keeping them out of his reach until he woke up shivering and groping for their smelly tails in the dark. The teasing wasn't the worst part of traveling with the wolves, it was hunger. Wolves could walk, kill, eat and sleep, then eat and sleep. This is what they did. Nana'b'oozoo could eat and sleep like a wolf but he could not do without eating for as long as a wolf could. At least he could look forward to a good feast once a week. In the meantime, he would nurse a bone or gnaw on a hide to stave off starvation. Not again would Nana'b'oozoo travel with wolves.

Snow was starting to melt away; spring warm winds were drawing the sap from the trees. Some of the summer birds began returning from their wintering grounds. They caroled, chirped, warbled away the wintry silence.

Nana'b'oozoo and his tutors came across a great river whose ice cover was breaking up into smaller, ever smaller slabs. Mother Wolf tilted her nose in the air; all the cubs did the same, sniffed deeply, loudly.

"What are you smelling for?" Nana'b'oozoo asked.

"Deer, on the other side!" said Wolf.

"How are we going to get on the other side?" the cubs wanted to know.

"My people have a way of crossing rivers during break-up," said Nana'b'oozoo.

"They do? The cubs asked wide eyed.

"Yes, they do," Nana'b'oozoo said. His brain was going into over-drive. He'd fix Wolf. He'd give her a good dunking. "What they do is this: they get a sapling, about fifteen steps long, about the size of your arm. When they are ready to cross the river they lay the sapling from the shore to the slab of ice. Once the man has his bridge in place, he crosses over and gets on board the next floe. Then he sets his pole-bridge on to the floe next. He keeps doing this until he gets to the far side. Do you understand?

"I want to go first!" the cubs yelped and squealed jumping up and down.

"No!" Mother Wolf growled. "It's too dangerous! Besides, you're too small. I'll go first."

They all looked for a nice pole and found one that was just the right size. First, Nana'b'oozoo showed her how to balance on a rolling log. Then she made five practice runs on the pole from the shore to the nearest floe back to the land without falling off. But she did teeter and totter. The cubs looked on, their hearts in their mouths one moment, laughing the next, and cheering when their mother passed the test.

Then came the real crossing. Wolf got on the log. It was an unsteady crossover. The cubs looked on, their fangs biting their claws, fearing that their mother would topple into the water. They cheered and woofed and howled when she made it to the next floe.

Half way across the river, Mother Wolf was flung off the pole and sank from sight. Nana'b'oozoo stifled a laugh to see such a sight; the cubs gasped and then whimpered.

"Don't worry!" Nana'b'oozoo tried to comfort the cubs. "Your mother is just bluffing; she's just playing a trick. She's hiding behind a chunk of ice. But she's not fooling me."

They called and called; the cubs were frantic. Nana'b'oozoo was put out with Wolf for playing such a dirty trick on him and her cubs.

"You stay here! Keep calling your mother! I'll go downstream a bit." So saying, Nana'b'oozoo left, heading downstream. Now and then he paused to glance over the river and to call out over the waters, "Neetauwiss!"

But no one answered.

On Nana'b'oozoo pressed. As he went along his anger changed to anxiety. He now called with deep worry.

Some distance downriver he heard someone answer, "Who are you looking for?"

"Wolf," Nana'b'oozoo yelled out.

"She's dead," said kingfisher, "when she fell into the water, the Great Lynx dragged her down into the depths. She'll never come back!"

Nana'b'oozoo was in rage. He thundered so that all could hear, "I'll go down! I'll go after Great Lynx. I'll put an end to him and bring back Wolf to us!" Then he cried.

NANA'B'OOZOO WEEK-OZHAEBUNAUN

Aupitchih Nana'b'oozoo nishkaudizeebun. Geesh-aendum wee auzhidaewauwaetoowaut. Washamae gee waenipunut dush tchi dooduming. Manitouwit Nanan'boozoo gee kishki-aewizih, gee mino-doodoowaun Anishinaubaen, waesseehnun, benaehnsiwun, geegoohnun, manitoushun gauh kotugiwaudjin weendigoon, matchiauwishun gayae; gee pishu-ozhaewaun gayae waegawaenun gayae gauh matchi doodoowaugawaenun bimigaedaugunun. Zaum gee naubaewih tchi auzhidaewauwaetoowaupun kaugaugheenun, aeshnbunun, gimoodinauhnun gayae gauh kitinimookodjin geegoohnmun.

Missowauh manitouwit kitchi-kishki-aewizit, inineewit w'gee gaushn-ih, gee-baedjeewee, washamae animooshuk gee noondumaewuk, washamae migiziwuk waussuh iko-waubiwuk, washamae waussuh animooshuk gee izhi-maundjigaewuk. Tchi baeshowitoowaut gauwisaungun aubidaek w'gee wiyaezhingae, geemootaugae, geewautisutaugae.

Ahneen gae-izhi-baeshi-witoowaupun zheezheebaehnun? Ahneen gae izhi-week-ozhaebunaupun?

Gauh iko nishi-baupinoodingibun waussaeyaubindumoowin manitoun gee auzhidaekaugoon, kauween w'gee zhawaenimikoosseen. Kauween gaego gee naubidussineenih tchi zhawaenimigoot.

Kauween mino-waubuminaugoozeeininik neegaun nakae gauh Nana'b'oozoo bimaudiziwin, wae-needjaunisidjik gee aungaummauwaun w'daunissiwaun "Kego baumaenimaukaegoon Nana'b'oozoowish. Kitimishkih. K'gah kitimaugis! K'gah pakadae!

Pigook-kaewiss w'daunissun w'gee weedigaemaun Nana'b'oozoon. W'gauh izhi aungaumimind gee izhi-issaemigut chibwauh kabik-issaemiguk neezh-geezis. Weedigaemaugunun gee weendumaugoon" Awo-ginoosh manitook, maudjeewish k'medawae-igun. Gee chaekau-kawung gawaek gee izhauh manitoowaunig aundih gauh dazhi ningumitoowaut manitoun, wauwaushkaeshiwun, aehnsebunun, kookidjeeshun, addikoon gayae w'needjaunissun, ozhishaenun gayae.

Gauh bizung-waubit Nana'boozoo gee bizindaun w'd'initaugooziwin ani-biziwaeshimoonik maegayauk, ahneen aen-itaugoonik.

"Ahneen w'ae-ondjih neenawi-taugooziwin, beebaugidaemo beebaug-daemut awiyah k'd'intaugooz?"

W'gee doosk-aubit, w'gee dautig-aubit, w'gee waubumaun odjidumoon numudinit tikwuning.

"Ondjih" gee maudjitauh Nana'b'oozoo, gee ani-nanigishkizih w'gauh izhi neena-waendung "needjaunisuk-daninaundumook ... N'daunawaewiss."

"Tuguh! Mashko-waendun! Nana'b'oozoo! Ahneen aen-indiyin? Mino-waungae-kunaumau, mino waewaekunau-gunug-idjeeg-kunaumauh-nawutch k'gah gazheekunaumauh-tibishko paupaussae inawaewae-igaet k'gah inawaewaekunaumauh owih daewae-igun.

Nana'b'oozoo w'gee baengiwung zeebeengawaehnsun gee maud-waewae-kunaumaut, washamae gazhee-waewaekunaumaun nawutch gazhee kauh.

"Nawutch onishishin!" Zaum k'geezheekauh! Kauween ae-apeetwaewae-aungishimoot benae k'gah apeet-kunaumaussee daewae-igun. Kauween awiyah w'dauh apeetch-kaudaessaessae ae-apeetaungizhi-oot benae.

Nana'b'oozoo gee medawaewae-igae maegawauh ningumoot.

"Mee igoh gawaek" Kittoh odjidumoozhish mee igoh gayae w'gee maudjitaut odjidumo-itaugoozit, gawau-kawaushkinit gayae. Atchinah gee auwaun mee weedji-odjitamoon w'gee abi-weedji-gaumikoot, gunkissaehsun gayae; gee dibaubumikoowaun weedji-waesseehniwaun.

"Ahneen aen-doodumaek," gagawaediwaewuk benaesheehnuk.

"Neemimim!"

"N'dauh neemimin nah gayae neeniwind?"

Ahneen nangae igoh nauh! Washamae dauh onishishin tchi neemiyaekoobun mitukummik dush metigoong; keeshpin bizozidaeshinook maegawauh neemiyaek kauween waussuh k'dauh pungishizeem. Washamae w'dauh onishishin gayae tchi boodoowae-yaekoobun, k'dauh geewitau-augoonugaum dush.

Gauh maudagaez-aendigik wee neemiwaut zaum waussuh gee ayauwuk Nana'b'oozoo tchi daeb-ibinaupun.

Nana'b'oozoo gee weendumoowaun "Keeshpin wauh neemiwaegawaen aubidaek w'dauh auwudoonauwauh missun ... kauween wee daewaegaessee. W' gee minisaewuk.

W'gauh mauwaundjistoowaut mino-minik missun w'gee boodoowaudumoowaut. Gauh gazheeyaukidaenik mee Nana'b'oozoo gee weendumoowaut wee kiki-inoomoowaut oshki-neemiwin "Bizungwaub-nugauwin" gauh izhi-nikaudung. "Bizungwaub-nugauwin," gauh izhi-nikaudung. "Waenipunut! Neezhing aetah dah weekidjitoonauwauh mee tchi kiki-aendumoowaut. Baezhigwun aetah ondjimaugaewin "Kauween k'gah waubusseem; k'gah augiweeng-gawaebizoom! K'nissitootaum nah?"

Kakinah w'gee nissitumook. "Aehn.:

Gauh maudwaewae-kunaumind daewae-igun mee gee maudji-kaudaessaewaut neemiwaewissuk, aegauch wiyae-oshkut kauween kiki-aenduzigoowah nakae wauh inugauwaut, aeshkum gazhee kaudae-ossauwaut w'gauh ani-ningudaendjigaewaut. Nawutch keeyaubih w'gee ani-waeweeb gee ani-paupau-wishimook. Paupau-ishimidjik w'pitaukooshkoodaudiwuk, w'gee pitauk-ozidaeshinook.

Gauh apeet-waewaek maumoowissing, daewae-igun, aenawaewae-ozidaeshinoowaut gaego.

Coocoocoo washamae gauh mino-ishaet gee munisoh bae-pekaun gae apeetawaewae-kunaundjigae Nana'b'oozoon gaego nishinaud-waewaekunaumaun daewaeginun. W'gee doskaubit mino-apee gee gaeski-waubumaut Nana'b'oozoon nawudinaunit zheesheebun, gabinaewaebinaunit, beemisko-gawaebunaunit, mee dush gee goondjidaunung kukizhaeng.

"Zhaemook! Zhaemook!" Noondaugoozih coocoocoo aeni-gook-gazheewaet. "Nana'b'oozoo k'nissikoonaun. Ningodjpuwaek! Ningodji-puwaedauh!"

Mee igo kakinah gee bauk-eengawaeniwaut. Naunoond-au-gooziwuk, zaegaewidumook geemeewaut, soosawae-puwaewaut.

Nana'b'oozoo aenigook chaunimizih, gee nishinaudjpugizoh wee nawudinung meedjim. Gee nawudinaun coocoocoon bimi-putoonit baeshoh, beemisko-quae-waewaebinaut coocoocoonish gabinaewaenind w'gee izhi-kaudaessae naunidauh gauh izhi-daebi-bidoot Nana'b'oozoo w'd'pikwauk-koonaun, gee zeend-kuhnzhee-waun, w'gee noondaugizinit mee gayae gee paginikoot. Mee dush noongoom wae-ondji-kishkitoot coocoocoo tchi beemisko-waewae-taut; maung bimi-puwaekuneen cheega-eeng; Nana'b'oozoo w'gee pissi-dayae-ishkawaut maungoon gauh apeech dayaeshkoowaut mee kaudaesun gee geekishkumiwaut nawutch ishkaworyaung. Gunkisaehnse gaweeniwiputoot gee zheebau-putooh beeto-kau-dung Nana'b'oozoon.

Nana'b'oozoo Gagawaedji-nawudinaut gunkisaehnsun pishig-binaun gee baeshaubeebinaun, keeyaubih ae-izhi-kiki-inoowauzin-augoozit noongoom. Tchi zhimugidjeeshkawaut amikoon inaukini-gaebun Nana'b'oozoo, w'gee mauhnzh-eewee, w'gee izhi-mugishku-moowaun zawaunigoom aetah. Kakinah gee waebeemikutinik meedjim.

Minik gauh medawaewae-igaet, gauh apeetch anookeet Nana' b'oozoo gee ayaekowee, pakadae gayae. Gee mukowaenimaut zhee-sheebimun. Minoziwidugaenuk, geezhi-oohnzoodaenuk, inaendum. Daupinung cheecheeg-kizhae-igun, Nana'b'zoo gee cheechee-gikizhae-ung boodoowaun. Kaukaukadae-igim kunun aetah gauh mukungin.